GAMBLING MAN

Jeff Blaine has been raised in Plainsville by his Aunt Beulah and Uncle Wirt from a baby, after his mother died in childbirth and his father Nate blew out of town. Twelve years later Nate returns, looking for a rest and a reconciliation with the son he never knew. But Nate's a gambler and a hellraiser — and upon learning that Jeff is following in his footsteps, Beulah spreads a simple but poisonous lie that ensures he disappears again, wanted for robbery and murder. When Jeff, now a young man, discovers his aunt's treachery, he vows never to forgive her. Then an old comrade of his pa's brings news: Nate is in Mexico, running from a firing squad. The only thing that will save him is five thousand dollars. And the only way to get it is by robbing a bank . . .

SPECIAL MESSAGE TO READERS

THE ULVERSCROFT FOUNDATION
(registered UK charity number 264873)
was established in 1972 to provide funds for research, diagnosis and treatment of eye diseases. Examples of major projects funded by the Ulverscroft Foundation are:-

- The Children's Eye Unit at Moorfields Eye Hospital, London
- The Ulverscroft Children's Eye Unit at Great Ormond Street Hospital for Sick Children
- Funding research into eye diseases and treatment at the Department of Ophthalmology, University of Leicester
- The Ulverscroft Vision Research Group, Institute of Child Health
- Twin operating theatres at the Western Ophthalmic Hospital, London
- The Chair of Ophthalmology at the Royal Australian College of Ophthalmologists

You can help further the work of the Foundation by making a donation or leaving a legacy. Every contribution is gratefully received. If you would like to help support the Foundation or require further information, please contact:

THE ULVERSCROFT FOUNDATION
The Green, Bradgate Road, Anstey
Leicester LE7 7FU, England
Tel: (0116) 236 4325

website: www.ulverscroft-foundation.org.uk

Gambling Man

Clifton Adams

First published in Great Britain by Fawcett
First published in the United States by Fawcett

First Isis Edition
published 2020
by arrangement with
Golden West Literary Agency

*A catalogue record for this book is available
from the British Library.*

ISBN 978–1–78541–858–7

Published by
Ulverscroft Limited
Anstey, Leicestershire

Set by Words & Graphics Ltd.
Anstey, Leicestershire
Printed and bound in Great Britain by
T. J. International Ltd., Padstow, Cornwall

This book is printed on acid-free paper

CHAPTER ONE

Plainsville had been a wonderful place to live in. Jefferson Blaine could remember it very well, although he had been a mere child then — eight or nine years ago. Now he was twelve and practically a man.

He had dreams of those old days sometimes, and in his sleep he could hear the harsh, strident laughter of the cowhands as they raced their horses through the dusty streets of the town, shooting off their guns and scaring the citizens half to death.

But they had never scared Jefferson Blaine, for in his adventurous young soul he had always been one of them, even though he was a town boy and had no horse to ride or Colt's to shoot. When they laughed, Jeff laughed. He would run into the street and wave to them, not at all afraid that the excited horses would trample him to death, as his Aunt Beulah often said they would.

There was one time in particular that he would never forget, and that was when a whooping cowboy had swooped him right off the ground and flung Jeff up behind the saddle. He had never felt so big in his life as he had that day, his arms hugging the big cowhand's waist as they made two complete runs of Main Street.

Aunt Beulah had heard about it, of course, and that night Uncle Wirt had dragged him behind the smoke-house and given him the breeching of his life. But he was never sorry about it. He'd have done it again, any time.

But the good old days were gone forever, Jeff thought sourly, trudging the path to Harkey's pasture, where the Sewell cow was kept. Every morning, even in the winter, he had to take Bessie to the pasture, and every evening he had to bring her back for milking; Aunt Beulah was dead set on having a cow for fresh milk and butter.

Far up the path another barefoot "cowboy" plodded toward the pasture to fetch the family cow, and at the foot of the path others were coming. The way it is now, Jeff thought bitterly, living in Plainsville wasn't like living in town and it wasn't like living on a ranch. It was just somewhere in between, the same as living nowhere.

At the pasture's barbed-wire gate Jeff cupped his hands to his mouth and bellowed, "S-o-o-o, Bessie!" He hoped the fool cow would have sense enough to come without his having to look for her. Several cows were right at the gate waiting to be taken home, but not Bessie. The fool critter was probably up to her knees in some bog and he'd have to go pull her out.

He cupped his hands and bellowed again, and after a while he saw Bessie's tan and white spotted hide moving through the stand of willows near the pond. This was his lucky day, he thought. But he did not feel elated.

Todd Wintworth, who was Jeff's age, was hazing his own family cow through the barbed-wire gate. Jeff scrunched down by a fence post to wait for Bessie. Todd came up to him swinging a piece of rope as if it were a lariat.

"You got Bessie trained pretty good," Todd said. "I had to go in after Blackie. Darn fool ain't got enough sense to know when it's time to eat."

The two boys sat on the ground, chewing the young grass thoughtfully. Below them lay the town, such as it was. The pasture lay on a gradual slope to the east, and now they had a bird's-eye view of Plainsville's tar-paper roofs and dusty streets. The houses were not much more than frame shacks, and not many of them were painted. Each house had its own little plot of ground for vegetables, and most of them had cowsheds and hen houses as well.

By golly, Jeff thought, it looks more like a ghost town than a place where fifty or sixty families live!

He turned his attention to the sun, now settling behind the western prairie. It was sluggish and red, like some enormous tick that had gorged itself with blood. He studied the pattern of woodsmoke coming from the tin stovepipes sticking through the tar-paper roofs and wondered what Aunt Beulah was fixing for supper.

Todd Wintworth jumped up suddenly and hurled a stone at his cow. "There, Blackie! Get back on the path!" He shrugged with disgust and looked at Jeff. "Guess I better go, else I'll be chasin' that fool clear up to the Territory. By the way, Amy wants to know if you're aimin' to come to her Japanese garden party tomorrow."

Amy was Todd Wintworth's sister, as pretty as a calendar picture, Aunt Beulah said, and Jeff was inclined to agree. Still, it made him feel kind of foolish having a girl tagging around after him the way Amy Wintworth did. They used to tease him about it at the academy, until he'd lost his temper and bloodied some noses. Lately, he had made a point of ignoring her when he thought somebody might be watching.

But secretly he was pleased that Amy was stuck on him. There were plenty of boys at the academy who wouldn't mind some teasing, if Amy Wintworth would just look in their direction.

He shrugged now, as though Amy Wintworth's party was a lot of fool kid stuff. But he said, "I'll think about it, maybe."

Todd heaved two more stones at the straying Blackie, then started the trek down the long slope. He was about twenty paces away when he stopped and called: "Say, I almost forgot. Who've the Sewell's got visitin' with them?"

Jeff blinked. "Visiting?"

"Sure. I saw a black horse tied at your cowshed when I came past. There was a man takin' in a saddle roll."

"I don't know about any visitors," Jeff said. "I haven't been home since the academy let out."

Todd called something that Jeff didn't understand, and then started running through the weeds to head Blackie back to the path. Whoever the visitor was, Jeff hoped Aunt Beulah had fixed company rations for supper, because all this traipsing back and forth to the pasture had made him hungry.

By this time Bessie had arrived at the gate. Jeff pushed a rope loop off the gate post and a section of the barbed-wire fence fell to the ground. He put the fence up again after the cow was out and followed Bessie's switching tail down the path to Plainsville.

Jeff soon forgot about the visitor that Todd Wintworth had mentioned. He turned his mind to remembering the rowdy, violent nights that had been Plainsville's before the cattlemen started avoiding the town.

Time was when the piano in Bert Surratt's saloon had been pounded half the night and could be heard from one end of town to the other. There had been hardly a night that you didn't hear gunfire. More than once old Abe Roebuck, the carpenter and town handyman, had been called out of bed in the middle of the night to go to work on a new pine burying box.

Oh, there had been excitement, all right, and Jeff didn't think he would ever forgive the squatters for ending it.

No more would the bawling, leather-lunged cowhands come storming into Plainsville, blowing in their pay and putting some life into the place. The big outfits like the Cross 4, the Big Hat, and the Snake, all said they'd be damned if they'd trade in a town where squatters were catered to. And from that time on they had taken their business to Yellow Fork, which was not as handy as Plainsville but at least was a place that understood cattlemen.

That was how Plainsville got to be a squatter town. It was rare to see a man wearing a revolver on Main Street any more, unless he was a traveler, and Jeff could remember when every man in town had a heavy Colt's slapping against his thigh. There were no more flashy cowhands with colorful neckerchiefs and bench-made boots and fancy rigs.

All you saw now were bib overalls and thick-soled boots or brogans, and if a man carried a gun at all, likely it would be a shotgun — which was just about as low as a man could sink.

Jeff trudged down toward the bottom of the slope, powdery red dust squirting up between his toes at every step. What I'm going to have when I grow up, he thought, is a pair of bench-made boots, with fancy stitching on the side. Not that he wasn't grown up now, but he had no money.

That was a detail that he would work out later. Now he thought about the boots. They would have built-up leather heels and soles as thin as paper, so that he would have the feel of the stirrup when he rode. He would have his initials on them, and maybe a butterfly stitched in red and green and yellow thread, although such doings were pretty fancy for a working cowhand. Maybe he'd skip the butterfly — he didn't want the other hands laughing at him.

He thought about those boots for a long while as he followed Bessie's eternally switching tail along the path. He was close enough to town to smell the woodsmoke from all the cookstoves, and it made him hungrier than ever. Just his initials on the boots would be enough. He hoped that Aunt Beulah would have fried chicken and gravy and biscuits, as they usually did when they had important company.

The horse was right where Todd Wintworth had said it was, the reins looped over the makeshift hitching rack by the cowshed. The animal was a real beauty, too; black as charcoal and well cared for. Jeff paid special attention to the tooled leather saddle, and to the well-rubbed boot which held a walnut-stocked Winchester. That was the kind of rig Jeff would have some day. His hands itched to ease that Winchester out of the boot and just feel it.

He kept glancing back at the horse and rig as he put Bessie in the stall and measured out a bucketful of feed. He was curious as to why a man who owned an outfit like that would be visiting with the Sewells.

Aunt Beulah put no store in guns of any kind, nor in men who carried them. Neither did Uncle Wirt, for that matter. He who lives by the sword shall die by the sword, they said. Not that it made any sense; in all Jeff's twelve years he had never once seen a man carry a sword in Plainsville.

But that was the way they were, especially Aunt Beulah. Whenever you did something she didn't like, she always had some scripture quote handy to prove that it was wrong.

Anyway, his chores for the day were over, unless there was some stovewood to be chopped. All that was left was the milking, and Uncle Wirt usually took care of that. Jeff took one last covetous look at the booted rifle and started for the house.

"Jefferson, have you got the cow stalled and the feed put out?"

It was his Aunt Beulah, who had just come to the kitchen door to peer out at him. She was a tight-knitted little woman with thinning gray hair and piercing gray eyes. The only time Jeff had ever seen any color in her face had been several years ago when she came down with the slow fever — all other times her face was as gray as lye-bleached leather.

Aunt Beulah's mouth reminded Jeff of a steel trap that had snapped shut on something, especially when she was mad or upset. And that was exactly the way her mouth looked now, like a steel trap, locked tight.

"Yes, ma'am," Jeff said, "Bessie's put up in the shed. Who we got visiting?"

"You didn't jog her down that path, did you?" Aunt Beulah asked, ignoring his question.

"No, ma'am," Jeff said, stamping the dust from his bare feet on the platform porch.

"I've seen some of them cowboys jogging them," Aunt Beulah said indignantly. "It's a sin and a crime to jog a cow when she's heavy with milk. Come on in. Supper will be on pretty soon."

Jeff stepped into a kitchen heavy with the rich aroma of frying chicken, and his mouth watered. Nobody in the world could cook like Aunt Beulah. He sure hoped the company, whoever it was, didn't like the gizzard, because that was his favorite part.

Now Jeff's attention was drawn again to his aunt, and he shuffled his feet uneasily on the scrubbed kitchen floor. He didn't like the tightness of her mouth and the sharp jutting of her small chin. He searched his mind for something that he had done wrong, but he could think of nothing — not anything recent.

Her mouth came open for just an instant, and then snapped shut almost immediately. She took his arm and turned him toward the parlor. "Come with me, Jefferson," she said shortly. "There's somebody you — you'll have to meet."

This was a pretty strange way for his aunt to act about company, Jeff was thinking, but he had learned long ago not to argue with her when she was like this. He walked willingly into the small, immaculate parlor.

His Uncle Wirt, a small man with drooping mustaches and a glistening bald head, was sitting very stiff and erect in one of the uncomfortable parlor chairs, as though someone were holding him there at the point of a gun. He blinked when Jeff came into the room and tried hard to relax.

"Jeff," he said, clearing his throat, "come on in. Here's somebody wants to see you."

To Jeff's way of thinking, Uncle Wirt seemed every bit as upset as Aunt Beulah. But he didn't give it a second thought when he saw the man sitting across the room from his uncle — a tall, dark-complexioned man with eyes as dark as an owl's, with shaggy black brows, and a mouth so full and wide that Jeff was briefly reminded of the catfish he sometimes caught in Carter's pond.

When the man stood up, the entire room seemed to grow in size. He said softly, "So you're Jeff!"

That was all he said, and he stood there with his arms hanging relaxed. Jeff didn't know what to say, so he said nothing.

Jeff could hear the old pendulum clock on the mantle ticking away the seconds, and still no one said a thing.

The instant the stranger stood up from his chair, Jeff vaguely realized that something was wrong. The picture was not quite complete. It was just a feeling he had that something was missing, but he couldn't put his finger on it until he saw the cartridge belt hanging on the hat tree in the hall. Then he knew what it was.

This man wore a gun.

Not in Aunt Beulah's house, he wouldn't, but you could see that he didn't feel quite right about the absence of that Colt's heavy weight on his hip. It was as obvious as a man going to church without his shirt.

There were men like that. Jeff could remember seeing two or three of them before, during the squatter trouble, when the big outfits were putting Territory guns on their payrolls. Not that this dark stranger was a Territory man, or an outlaw, or anything like that. He didn't have that mean, hunted look that men get when they've run too far and too long. Still, Jeff couldn't imagine what this man was doing in his Aunt Beulah's and Uncle Wirt's house.

At last the stranger said, "Miss Beulah, ain't you going to tell the boy who I am?"

Aunt Beulah's face was grayer than Jeff had ever seen it, and her grim mouth was clamped tight. Finally Uncle Wirt stirred uneasily.

"Jeff," he said, "this here's your pa."

It made so little sense that Jeff would have thought that his uncle was joking, except that Uncle Wirt never joked about anything. This black-eyed stranger was his pa?

The man said in that same quiet voice, "Don't you have anything to say, Jeff?"

Jeff cleared his throat. He had never been in a situation like this before — he was afraid the stranger was funning him. At last he spoke up, his voice amazingly loud.

"I guess you got the wrong boy, mister. My pa's dead."

A cloud crossed the man's eyes as he looked at Aunt Beulah. "Did you tell him I was dead, Miss Beulah?"

Jeff's aunt glanced at her husband. "No, I didn't!" she snapped.

"That's funny, ain't it? I wonder where he got the idea?"

"I told Jefferson you was likely dead," Aunt Beulah replied sternly. "What did you expect us to think, after twelve years?"

The stranger stood for a moment, very still. Then in four giant strides he crossed the room and stood in front of Jeff. "My name," he said, "is Nathan Blaine. Some call me Nate. A little more than twelve years ago I married the prettiest girl in southwest Texas. She was your Aunt Beulah's baby sister — Lilie Burton her name was before we were married. Lilie was your mother, Jeff. And I'm your pa. Do you want to shake hands?"

Jeff couldn't take his gaze from the stranger's face. He said, "You ain't funnin' me, are you, mister?"

"Ask your uncle, Jeff. Ask your aunt."

"I never saw you before! How could you be my pa?"

Jeff turned his gaze to his aunt and saw that it was true. He felt strange and kind of choked, and he didn't know exactly what to do. The stranger was holding out his big, lean hand, and Jeff stared at it for maybe two or three long ticks of the mantle clock.

Then they shook hands.

CHAPTER TWO

Supper was an uneasy affair. For the first time since Jeff could remember, Uncle Wirt didn't talk about the tin shop, and Aunt Beulah didn't mention once that she was afraid the skunks were going to get at her chickens. They pitched into the chicken and gravy as if it were a matter of life and death. Nathan Blaine asked Jeff about his studies at the academy, but pretty soon the talk died away, strangled in the tense atmosphere.

Afterward, Nathan prowled the tiny parlor, and finally he said, "Think I'll go over to town for a while, and see how the old place has changed." He looked at Jeff. "How'd you like to come along, Jeff?"

"Too late for a boy to be traipsing about," Aunt Beulah put in firmly.

"Oh," Nathan said quickly, drawing himself a little taller. "Yes, I guess it is. Well, maybe tomorrow, boy."

Then he bolted, as though the house were choking him. He grabbed his revolver from the rack and buckled it as another man would put on a hat. "Don't wait up for me," he said. "I'll spread my roll in the kitchen."

After he had left, Jeff said, "Aunt Beulah, why didn't you tell me about —"

"He's your pa," his aunt snapped. "You might as well call him that. I didn't tell you about him because I didn't know anything to tell. He ran off from you when you were just a baby. It's the Lord's working that you didn't dry up and die, like your mother, and I guess you would have if it hadn't been for me and your Uncle Wirt."

She turned and went to the kitchen. In a minute she was back with a pan full of green beans to be snapped. "Ain't you gone to bed yet?"

"I was going," Jeff said wearily.

He went out to the back porch and washed his dusty feet in a bucket of water that had been set out for that purpose. He had to lather them good and scrub hard because Aunt Beulah would inspect them before she let him get between her clean sheets. He heard his Uncle Wirt come in from the front gallery and say:

"Well, he's headed straight for Bert Surratt's."

Aunt Beulah snorted. "Where did you expect he'd head for?"

Jeff could almost see his uncle's shrug of uneasiness. "I was hoping he'd changed, but I guess he hasn't. The way he wears that gun — I don't like it. That's something new since we saw him last."

"Twelve years," Aunt Beulah said, "and gone downhill all the way, if you ask me."

"Now, Beulah, don't be too tough on him. He took it harder'n most when Lilie passed on. We got no way of knowing what things goes on in a man's mind at a time like that."

Jeff could hear the beans thudding against the side of the tin pan as his aunt snapped them expertly and quickly, the way she did all things.

"Twelve years," she said again. "Seems to me that's enough time to get over what was bothering him. Lilie was my baby sister, remember, but I got over it."

"I'm not standing up for him, but —" Then Jeff came into the room and Uncle Wirt was suddenly quiet.

"Let me see your feet," Aunt Beulah said.

Jeff had a thousand questions to ask, but he knew they would get no answers. He trudged to his room when his aunt had finished her inspection.

He lay in bed straining his ears to hear what his aunt and uncle were saying, but they were being careful and keeping their voices low. He thought, I wish I could have gone to town with him.

He'd never seen the inside of Bert Surratt's saloon, and that would have been something to brag to Todd Wintworth about. He'd heard tell of gambling and drinking and all kinds of carrying on, but you couldn't be sure unless you'd actually seen it.

Aunt Beulah was dead set against Bert Surratt, and so was Uncle Wirt. They were both good church-going people, and they hated drinking about as much as they hated anything. Jeff closed his eyes and tried to imagine what his father could be doing in a place like Surratt's.

He imagined a scene of painted dancing girls and piano music and lots of laughing and maybe a cowhand shooting at the ceiling with his Colt's revolver.

But he knew that it wasn't really that way. He had passed in front of Surratt's place many a time and hardly ever heard a sound, except maybe some casual talk and the click of a roulette ball.

He listened to the night and let vagrant thoughts drift through his mind.

There was that business at the Wintworth's. Lemonade and gingercakes and paper lanterns hanging on clothes-line poles in the Wintworth back yard — that was what they called a Japanese garden party in Plainsville. And there were always a lot of girls, too, wanting to play some fool game or other. Certainly he had outgrown kid stuff like that long ago.

He'd be expected to take a present, because it was Amy Wintworth's eleventh birthday. Whatever the present cost, sure as shootin' Uncle Wirt would take it out of the dime he got every two weeks for working at the tin shop and bringing in the cow.

After a while he got to thinking about Amy, and the party didn't seem so bad. He remembered seeing some Indian gewgaws in Baxter's store; bright colored beads and horn knitting needles and all kinds of stuff that Sam Baxter had got off an Indian trader up in the Territory. Indian stuff was pretty scarce in Texas now, and women seemed to take a shine to anything that was scarce. Maybe he'd ask Mr. Baxter how much the gewgaws cost.

Now Jeff became aware of the talk in the other room. Aunt Beulah and Uncle Wirt were still at it and had unconsciously raised their voices.

"It's that pistol that bothers me," Uncle Wirt was saying. "To look at him you'd think he was afraid of appearin' indecent without he had that gun strapped around his middle. Beulah, do you reckon he's in trouble?"

"Nathan Blaine has always been a trouble and a worry," Aunt Beulah answered shortly. "The older he gets, the bigger his troubles grow. That's the way it is with his kind."

Jeff could hear the parlor rocker squeaking, and he could almost see his aunt pushing rapidly back and forth, as she always did when she was upset.

"Maybe we oughtn't jump at conclusions," Uncle Wirt said thoughtfully. "Maybe he's been down south where a strapped gun is still the normal thing."

Jeff's aunt snorted. "I can tell by looking at him how much downhill he's gone. If he's robbed or killed somebody, I guess it wouldn't surprise me much."

"Beulah!"

"I mean it, every word!"

The rocker stopped for a moment, then started again harder than ever. "But I guess it's too late to do anything for Nathan Blaine," she added grimly. "It's the boy I'm worrying about. It scares me to think what evil influence he could work on Jeff if he ever got a hold on the boy."

"I don't think we have to worry about that," Uncle Wirt said. Jeff could imagine them looking knowingly at each other, thinking each other's thoughts.

It was a tough idea to get used to, Jeff was thinking, as he lay awake in his bed.

The tall man with the dark eyes was his pa, all right. Aunt Beulah had owned to that herself. Still, after twelve years, the idea took some getting used to.

Jeff's room was a small lean-to affair that had been added to the Sewell house long ago, when he got big enough to have a room of his own. Jeff lay staring out his window, listening to the muffled night sounds that hung over Plainsville. He wondered why his aunt didn't like his pa, and why her small eyes glinted every time she looked at Nathan Blaine. And, for the first time since he could remember, Jeff thought about his mother.

Lilie Blaine had died when Jeff was born. There was an old daguerreotype picture of his mother that had stood on the parlor library table ever since he could remember, so he knew pretty well what she had looked like. But practically nothing had been told him of his father. Wirt Sewell was his father — that's the way the Plainsville folks thought of it, and the way Jeff had thought of it too.

Where had Nathan Blaine, his real pa, been?

Nathan must have left Plainsville right after Lilie Blaine had died. And nobody around these parts had seen hide nor hair of him since. Jeff would have heard about it.

Jeff decided that he liked the idea of having a pa of his own. He had never given it much thought before — it was surprising how much pleasure it gave him. He didn't try to explain it, and it didn't make much difference that Nathan had deserted him twelve years ago. He was just glad that his pa had decided to come back to Plainsville.

Jeff was still awake when the whack of built-up heels sounded on the clay walk in front of the Sewell house.

Nathan Blaine's spurs made tinkling silver sounds in the night, and for a moment Jeff was reminded of the cow-hands that he had once admired so much. He remembered that very afternoon he had wished for boots exactly like the ones his pa was wearing, and he had thought what fun it would be to race through Plainsville on a painted horse and maybe shoot off his Colt's at the ceiling of Surratt's saloon.

A lot had happened since then.

Nathan Blaine was standing on the front gallery now. Jeff could see him through the window. He stood there, a tall, dark man against the night, as though he were trying to make up his mind to go inside where Aunt Beulah and Uncle Wirt were waiting. He made a small sound, almost like a groan, and opened the door.

"You back already, Nathan?" Uncle Wirt asked with false heartiness. Jeff heard the whack of something solid on wood, and he knew that his pa had hung up his revolver.

Nathan said mildly, "Nothing much to the town this time of night."

"Bert Surratt's still open, though, I guess," Aunt Beulah said pointedly.

"Yes," Jeff's pa said, and his voice sounded tired. "Bert's still open. How's the boy?"

"Jefferson is asleep." It was Uncle Wirt this time, and his voice was not quite so hearty. "Why don't you sit down, Nathan. We can talk a spell before bedtime."

"About me?"

"Well — Yes, I guess so, Nathan. Beulah and me was wondering, kind of — Well —"

“You were wondering why I came back to Plainsville, and what I intend to do about my boy?” Nathan Blaine’s voice was practically toneless, but there was a sting to it and Jeff could feel it. “I reckon,” he went on, “your answers will have to come from Jeff. Now I think I’ll spread my roll, if you don’t mind.”

That had been over an hour ago, and Jeff was still awake. His uncle and aunt had gone to bed in their room on the other side of the house, and his pa had spread his roll in the kitchen.

Doggone it! Jeff found himself thinking, why can’t they leave him alone?

CHAPTER THREE

There was strangeness in the air. Jeff couldn't explain it, but Plainsville had changed since Nathan Blaine rode into town. Things were not the way they used to be.

Not that Jeff let it worry him much. He was just beginning to get used to the idea of having a pa of his own, and he liked it. Especially when he compared Nathan to the other men in town. Nate had been in town three days now and Jeff's reaction toward his father had changed rapidly through several phases, from disbelief, to acceptance, to what was now a bursting pride.

Nathan was the kind of man a boy could be proud of. Here was no plodding small-town storekeeper like Sam Baxter, no timid businessman like Jed Harper. Nate Blaine was cut to no particular pattern; no set of cut-and-dried rules controlled him.

In a crowd Nate stood out like black against white and all others became shadowy and indistinct. He had a way of throwing back his big head and looking down with vague contempt upon the tallest man. There was a breath of danger about him that was not entirely due to the guns he wore.

It was all too clear that Nathan did not care a tinker's damn whether he was liked, but he demanded respect and he got it, no matter how grudgingly.

It was the morning after Nate's arrival that Jeff first began to experience these new sensations of pride and importance. Aunt Beulah was particularly grim and snappish that morning. "Jefferson," she said shortly, halfway through breakfast, "it's time you got started to the pasture with Bessie."

"Gee, I'm not through with my flapjacks yet!"

"Well, don't dawdle. You'll be late for school."

It was strange how she could serve up flapjacks and pork sausage to Nathan and still pretend that he wasn't there. Nate sat smiling faintly all through the meal, speaking occasionally to Wirt or Jeff. If he was aware of the chill behind Beulah's eyes, he did not show it. "No need to hurry, son," he said pleasantly. "I'll get my horse saddled and we can ride to the pasture, if you don't mind doubling up."

Jeff could hardly believe that Nathan, even though he was his father, would let him ride that fine black animal. "Do you mean it?"

"Sure I do." Nathan stood up from the table, that quiet smile still touching the corners of his mouth. "That was a fine breakfast, Beulah, and I'm grateful. Now if you'll excuse me . . ." He nodded to Beulah and. Wirt and walked out to the cowshed.

Eagerly, Jeff pushed his plate away and started to follow his father.

"Finish your breakfast," Aunt Beulah said sternly.

"But you told me to hurry!"

"Never mind. Stay right here and clean your plate."

Uncle Wirt looked kind of funny, but he said nothing. Reluctantly, Jeff pulled the plate back and finished the flapjacks as quickly as possible, thinking how unpredictable his aunt could be when she took the notion. One minute she was hurrying him, the next minute she was trying to detain him. Out of pure orneriness, he thought bitterly, just to keep me from riding that black horse.

Then a strange thing happened when he finally finished his plate to Aunt Beulah's satisfaction. "Jefferson," she said, stopping him as he hurried for the back door, "I want to tell you something." Suddenly she put her thin, hard arms around him and held him hard, something she hadn't done since he was very young. "We love you, Jefferson," she said tightly. "You're all we've got, me and Wirt."

It was very strange, and it made Jeff uncomfortable. He was no baby. He didn't like having women paw at him.

"I've got to get started with Bessie," he said, twisting away.

Nathan had already turned the cow out and was in the saddle. "You ready?" he asked. Then he kicked out a stirrup and swung Jeff up behind. The animal's flanks were sleek and warm, and the saddle leather creaked luxuriously as Jeff settled himself behind his father. "Gee," he said in awe, "I'll bet this is the best horse in Texas."

Nate Blaine laughed abruptly. "You might not be far wrong."

Jeff would not soon forget that morning, especially the looks of envy that other barefoot cowboys shot up at them. And later, as they rode through streets of Plainsville to the academy, it seemed that everybody stopped for a moment to watch them.

There goes Nate Blaine and his boy, they were saying. Suddenly the name of Blaine had become something to be proud of.

Jeff became more aware of this as one moment followed another. Suddenly people looked at him differently. He was "young Blaine," Nate Blaine's boy.

That afternoon he found his pa waiting for him near the head of Main Street.

"You finished with your studies at the academy, son?" Nathan asked.

"For today I am. You waiting for somebody?"

"That's right. What do you aim to do for the rest of the day?"

Jeff's heart beat a little faster. Maybe his pa was going to let him ride behind the saddle again. "I guess I'll go after Bessie, like always."

"You mind if I ride along?"

It was then that Jeff saw his pa's black hitched at the watering trough. Beside the black there was a sleek bay mare, her coat recently brushed and gleaming like a new dollar. "I got the mare at the public corral," Nathan said. "She's yours for the rest of the day, son — if you feel like ridin', that is."

Jeff found that he could not speak. Of course he had ridden horses, but not very often. Just enough to whet his appetite for it, and he had hardly ever seen a horse, even Phil Costain's old dray nag, that his thighs didn't ache to feel a saddle between them. He looked quickly at his pa to make sure that he wasn't joking.

Nathan smiled. "Climb up, son. We'll ride to the pasture together."

There was nothing in the world, Jeff thought, like riding a good horse to make a man feel like a man! He felt the saddle, cured by sweat and by a hundred soapings to a rich tobacco brown. He climbed up on the mare and felt nine feet tall as he surveyed the town from his lofty position in the saddle.

Nathan Blaine said nothing, but laughed quietly. He reined his black into the street, and Jeff put the bay around and rode beside him.

Jim Lodlow, a scholar at the academy with Jeff, was standing in front of Baxter's store as they rode past. Jeff felt a bubbling inside and had a crazy impulse to giggle. Look at Jim Lodlow bugging his eyes!

But Jeff only nodded as they rode past, as though to imply that he was used to riding fine bay mares every day of the week. The fact that his bare feet did not quite reach the stirrups didn't bother him at all.

They reached the pasture in practically no time, and Jeff guessed that they could wait a while before calling Bessie. Besides, he was just getting the feel of the saddle and hated the thought of climbing down and letting down the barbed-wire gate.

His pa had a curious, faraway look in his dark eyes as he looked out at that cleared, fenced land.

"I can remember," Nathan said slowly, "when there wasn't a foot of barbed wire in this part of Texas.

Blackjack corrals and a few rawhide branding pens were all the fences we had."

Jeff had not thought of his father as an old man, and still didn't. Things just happened fast in Texas. It seemed that the squatters had come overnight, almost, and had hemmed the big outfits in and pushed them back toward the hills to the north.

But Nathan Blaine remembered when Sam Baxter's store was the only one around. The dry run to the east of town had been a flowing stream then, and a man from Kansas had put up a water wheel and ground flour on the shares. Those two buildings and a blacksmith shop had been all there was to Plainsville in those days, before the big out-fits began coming here and the town started to grow.

Jeff found himself listening with interest to what his pa had to say. It gave him a funny feeling to remember he was twelve years old and knew practically nothing about his own father.

Jeff said, "That must have been a long time ago."

"Yes, I guess it was. I was about the age you are now, I guess, when my family started down from Missouri to settle in Texas. Not much more than squatters we were, if the truth were told. My ma was set on getting the family a piece of land and living on it. She never did get the land, though, that she had wanted so much."

"Why not?" Jeff wanted to know.

Nathan Blaine turned his head slowly and gazed to the north. "Osages," he said. "White trash had them stirred up and they were raiding settler wagons coming through the Territory."

"Your ma was killed?"

"And two brothers. Me and my pa were the only ones to get to Texas, finally. Not that it did us much good."

"Why not?"

Nathan looked at his son. "Never mind. It's not important now."

Man and boy, they sat their horses proudly and gazed thoughtfully into the distance.

"Would you like to ride a piece down the fence?" Nathan asked.

And Jeff said, "I don't care," meaning that he was itching to.

They touched their horses and rode along the stretched barbed wire. Beyond was a stand of cottonwood marching green and proud across the prairie, following the banks of the narrow stream called Crowder's Creek.

The sun was still an hour away from the western edge of the world, and they rode all the way to Crowder's Creek before pulling up. "There used to be yellow cats down there," Nathan said, gazing down at the ripply ribbon of water.

"There aren't any more," Jeff complained. "The squatters built fish dams upcreek and cleaned them out. Were you in Plainsville when the hands from the big outfits used to come in to trade?"

"Yes. The town was different then."

"I remember," Jeff said, nodding, and Nathan Blaine smiled that thin smile of his.

Suddenly Jeff's pa threw himself out of the saddle and walked a little way toward the stream. Staring out past the creek, he said, "I guess I wouldn't be much surprised if you didn't like me. I sure haven't been much of a pa to you, and that's the gospel."

Jeff was surprised that the talk had taken this kind of turn. He would have preferred to keep it impersonal. Now he felt uncomfortable, as though he had done something wrong, and he didn't know exactly what kind of reaction was expected of him.

"I never said I didn't like you."

He thought he saw his pa stand just a little straighter.

"Well, you've got a right to, and I don't deny it. I guess I can't rightly explain just why I ran off from you when you was just a tyke. I've thought about it at times — but I don't know."

He was still looking across the creek, as though he spotted something interesting on the other side. But he went on in the same quiet, thoughtful voice.

"Once several years ago I was down south with the Mexicans, and right out of the clear it dawned on me that I'd had enough chasing, and what I really wanted was to come back to Plainsville and see my boy. That very night I got packed and rode clear up from Chihuahua. Then, when I got about an hour's ride from town, I turned around and went back again. I don't know just why I did it."

Jeff said nothing, for he knew that his father expected no answer. This was the first time a grown person had ever talked to him like an adult. It was flattering in a way, and he was proud to be talked to as an equal; but still it was confusing.

Then Nathan Blaine turned away from the creek and looked at his son. "Well, I'm glad you don't hate me, anyway. That's about all I can rightly expect." Suddenly he smiled, and walked over and stroked the bay's neck. "That's enough talk about me for a spell. Jeff, why don't you tell me about yourself?"

He didn't ask, "Have you been a good boy?" or "Do you have a girl?" or "Do you like your teacher?" Jeff hated those questions, and they were the ones adults always asked.

Not Nathan Blaine. He had come right out and asked, "Tell me about yourself." Man to man.

It gave the boy a warm feeling to be taken in and treated as though he had some sense, even though he was only twelve.

"Well," he said importantly, "I'm pretty good at figures at the academy. Uncle Wirt says I'll be taking over the tin shop books before long, if I keep it up."

"I see. What else are you good at, Jeff?"

"I'm a pretty good tin worker; Uncle Wirt teaches me a lot of things about it. I made a bucket for Aunt Beulah that she says is the best she ever saw, and I can roll and rivet stovepipe as good as anybody."

Nathan Blaine continued to stroke the bay's neck, but he no longer looked up at his son. "Your uncle taught you all that?"

"Sure," Jeff said. "He taught me to braid rawhide lariats, and make slingshots and willow whistles — a lot of things. He's been pretty good to me, I guess."

There was a sagging to Nathan Blaine's face, and suddenly he stopped stroking the bay and clinched his fist as though he were about to hit someone. "So your uncle taught you a lot of things, did he?"

Jeff didn't like the look on his pa's face. He wasn't smiling now. He looked grim and almost angry.

"Well," Nathan said, "here's something I'll bet he never taught you. Do you see that glistening stone across the creek, just at the edge of the cottonwood shade?"

Puzzled, Jeff nodded. The stone looked about the size of a buggy hub.

Nathan Blaine's hand moved almost faster than the eye could follow. As if by magic, his Colt's .45 jumped from his holster to his hand. The revolver exploded twice in quick succession, and Jeff stared dumbly as the glistening rock on the other side of the creek leaped into the air like a frightened cottontail.

Nathan's dark eyes were blazing as he wheeled to face his son. "Your Uncle Wirt never taught you to do a thing like that, did he?"

Jeff swallowed hard. He discovered that his voice was missing; he could make no sound. He shook his head.

"I didn't think so," his pa said proudly. "You don't see shooting like that around Plainsville, do you?"

Still dumb, Jeff shook his head again.

"Well, where I've been you have to learn to shoot that way or you don't stay alive." His mouth was not so grim now, and some of the fire left his eyes. He laughed shortly. "I didn't scare you, did I?"

At the very bottom of his stomach Jeff found his voice. "No. It didn't scare me a bit!"

"That's good," his pa said. "I'd hate to think a Blaine let himself be scared by a little noise."

It seemed to Jeff that he could still hear the sound of those shots rolling through the cottonwoods. It had not sounded like the cowhands shooting off their guns as they raced their horses through Plainsville. This had been sudden. And there had been no laughter to go with it.

"One of these days," Nathan told his son, "I'll show you how it's done. Let me see your hands."

Jeff held out his hands, and his pa whistled softly. "Good and big. That's good. You need big hands to squeeze the butt and catch the hammer." He held the revolver out to the boy, butt first. "Would you like to try it?"

Jeff blinked in disbelief. He had seen guns all his life, of course, but he had never had a chance to hold one.

"You mean I can shoot it?"

"Surc." His pa laughed. "Go on, take it."

Eagerly, Jeff reached for the revolver. Then, with the suddenness of lightning, the revolver blurred in Nathan Blaine's hand and the butt smacked into his palm. Hammer cocked, the muzzle snapped into position directly in front of Jeff's startled eyes.

Jeff had never known pure terror before that moment, with the muzzle so close to his nose that he could smell the burned powder, could feel the heat of the smoking barrel. He felt the blood drain from his face.

Nathan Blaine said, "The muzzle of a gun is not a pretty thing to look into, is it?"

His voice was deadly serious as he lowered the revolver. "Well, that's the first lesson a man has to learn, Jeff, if he wants to stay alive. Don't let yourself get in a position like that again."

Nathan held the revolver as he had before, by the barrel, upside down, butt extended forward. With one finger hooked in the trigger guard, he gave the gun a flip with his other fingers and wrist. The butt snapped into his palm and the hammer came back on the crook of his thumb at the same moment, and the gun was ready to fire.

"That's called the road agents' spin by some," Nathan said. "It's sudden death in any language. There's only one way to disarm a man, and that's to make him drop his gun to the ground. When a gunshark makes to hand you his gun, even when it's butt first, you're just a split second away from death."

Jeff cleared his throat. "I'll — I'll remember."

"I know you will." Nathan Blaine smiled quietly. "Do you still want to try it?"

Jeff stared at his father as though he had never seen him before. The boy was not afraid of him, but he understood that the dark look of danger was never far behind Nathan Blaine's black eyes.

"Do you mean it?" Jeff asked.

"I mean it. No tricks this time."

Jeff jumped from the saddle and took the heavy revolver. That thing of glued steel and polished walnut seemed almost alive, and he had never known that such a thrill of power could come from merely holding a cold, inanimate object. He had not guessed, either, that a .45 could be so heavy. He could hardly keep his arm from trembling as he held the revolver out in front of him.

"What'll I shoot at?"

Nathan laughed. "It makes no difference; you won't hit it anyway. This is just to show you what it feels like to have a gun go off in your hand."

Jeff picked out a cottonwood trunk across the creek. He had to wrestle the hammer back with both hands; then he held the revolver in front of him, aimed it and pulled the trigger.

He had not been prepared for the violent reaction in his hand. He almost dropped the gun. He could feel the shock of the explosion all the way to his shoulder. When the hammer fell, his gun hand leaped up almost over his head, and the roar was deafening.

He had no idea where the bullet went, but the cottonwood was standing solid and unshaken.

"Try it again," Nathan said mildly.

This time Jeff was better prepared for the violence of the recoil. He planted his bare feet solid on the ground, raised his arm slowly and sighted along the barrel, but after the explosion there was no sign that he had hit anything on the other bank. There wasn't even a spray of dust to show where the bullet hit the ground.

"Once more," his pa said quietly. "This time don't pull the trigger with your finger; just squeeze the butt with your whole hand."

Jeff tried it the way his pa said, and this time he was delighted to see dirt kick up near the base of the cottonwood.

"Not bad!" his father said, taking the revolver. He punched out the empty cartridge cases and reloaded the chambers with five rounds from his belt. The hammer went down on the empty chamber and the Colt's went into its holster.

"Could I try it again?" Jeff asked eagerly. "I bet I could hit it the next time!"

But Nathan shook his head. "You've had enough for one day. Just think over what I told you — that'll do you more good than burnin' up a wagonload of ammunition."

Jeff noticed that his pa was smiling and seemed to be in high spirits. "Yes, sir," he said, stepping up to the saddle, "Wirt Sewell is all right as a tinsmith, I guess, but I'll bet he can't teach you to shoot the way your pa can!"

"Shucks," Jeff said, "Uncle Wirt doesn't even own a gun."

Nathan Blaine laughed. And from the sound, it was easy to tell that he was not a man who laughed often. But now he looked upon his boy with a gentleness that was surprising; the tense line of his mouth was relaxed and the fire behind his eyes was almost invisible.

Jeff climbed up on the bay feeling more a man than he had ever felt in his life. He had felt a good horse between his legs, he had felt the buck of a .45 in his hand, and he had heard a savage music more enticing than a siren's song.

He rode erect and proud beside the tall figure of his pa.

Nathan was still smiling to himself when they reached the pasture gate. Jeff was put out because this was the one day that Bessie had to be waiting at the gate for him, robbing him of his chance to ride after her on his fine bay mare.

"Seems to me that mare's taken a liking to you, son," Nathan said. "What do you say I make arrangements to keep her for a while?"

Jeff knew that his eyes were bugging. "You really mean it?"

"Sure I mean it. Look, we'll have a fine time together. Why, you'll be the best rider and the best pistol shot in this part of Texas when your pa gets through with you. And I'll teach you other things, too. Things your Uncle Wirt never even heard about!"

Jeff was stupified with pleasure. A fine horse to ride all the time! A real Colt's revolver to shoot! Who could tell, maybe his pa would even buy him some thin-soled boots. It seemed that all good things had come at once!

They jogged Bessie almost all the way home. Aunt Beulah was going to raise ned when she found out about it, but Jeff didn't care. Within Jeff's chest there was a kind of pleasant swelling he had never known before. And once his pa reached out and punched him very gently on the shoulder, grinning. It was the only time Nathan had touched him, except for that cool handshake when they had first met in Aunt Beulah's parlor.

CHAPTER FOUR

At one time or another during his span of thirty years Nathan Blaine had tried his hand at many things. He had mauled spikes with a railroad construction gang in Missouri, hired out as a soldier with Mexican revolutionaries, trailed cattle to Wichita and Dodge. He had traveled the whole Southwest trading horses, he had served as special marshal at an end-of-track shantytown in Indian Territory. At times he had been with the law, at times against it, depending on which current he was drifting with.

His profession now was gambling.

He had learned his trade in many schools and from many teachers. He had plied his art in cow camps and on the trail, in the deadfalls of Dodge, around mess fires of the Mexican Army, unconsciously increasing his knowledge of faro, stud, twenty-one and all the other gambling games.

His natural aptitude for cards was excellent; he had patience, stamina, an alert brain and a long memory. He had never used a holdout harness, and he never wore one of those deadly little derringers tucked away in his vest.

He depended on his skill and knowledge of cards to provide a winning margin in poker, as he depended on his nerve and speed with guns to provide the winning margin in a far more deadly game.

Nathan Blaine could not recall the exact moment when his handling of cards and firearms had acquired the polish of a professional. His school had been a violent one and only the quickest and the toughest had lived — there was a grave in Sonora to mark the success of his first examination, and another in the Indian country, near the end-of-track shantytown, and in New Mexico still another.

There were many places in the Southwest where the name of Nathan Blaine had meaning and was respected and even feared. He had hoped that Plainsville would be different.

This was a town of squatters who never looked beyond their own barbed-wire fences. He had returned to Plainsville just because it was the kind of place it was. To tell the truth, he was tired and needed rest.

Now he sat day after day in Bert Surratt's saloon, stark and bleak as a squatter's barn, turning a dollar now and then with the "grangers," as the newspapers were beginning to call them. When he fled the town twelve years ago, he hadn't thought he would ever return. When Lilie died he had not imagined that the black despair would ever lift, or that some day he would want to look upon the baby that had killed her.

He had never amounted to much in Plainsville. A livery boy, a part-time rider for the big outfits. Only Lilie had believed in him, had seen anything in him.

And when Lilie died . . .

He remembered that day all too well; all the grief and helpless rage that had followed him down the years. His wife was dead. The baby — his son — had killed her. In the darkness of his soul he had craved violence, he had longed to lash out and cause hurt, as he had been hurt. But how could a man hurt a baby; how could a man direct all the hate in his brain against his own new-born son? Yet Nathan could not bear to look at that small, red face; so he had left Plainsville and his son behind, taking his wildness and rage with him.

But now he was back.

He sat at one of Surratt's plank tables riffling a deck of cards over and over in his hands, waiting for someone to come in and start a game. It was a slow way to make a living, being a gambler in a place like Plainsville.

If it wasn't for the boy, he thought, I'd pack up and leave right now!

He'd have to keep clear of the New Mexico country, of course, because he'd heard the marshals were looking for him over there. But there were plenty of other places. If worst came to worst he could always head back for Sonora or Chihuahua — or Indian Territory. The Federal court at Fort Smith wasn't as powerful as it used to be, so the Territory might be a pretty good place.

But Nathan could hardly believe the hold his son had got on him. He had not been prepared to find so much of Lilie in the boy. Even now, after all these years, the sound of her name could squeeze his heart dry, leaving him bloodless and cold, savage with loneliness.

Bert Surratt, the only other person in the place, came over to Nathan's table and took a chair. The saloonkeeper was a beefy man in his late fifties, an early settler.

"Slow today."

"Every day's slow."

"Maybe Plainsville will get the railroad," the saloonkeeper speculated. "There's been talk in that direction."

"It's just talk," Nathan said. "Why would a railroad want to lay track out here to the very center of God's nowhere?"

Surratt shrugged. "Well, there's still plenty of cattle around here, if you can get to them through the barbed wire. The town would make a fine shipping center for this part of Texas."

Nathan gazed without interest at the dirty, flyspecked mirror behind the bar. "Don't you believe it. Plainsville will go on dying until some day they'll have to bury it to keep it from smelling."

The saloonkeeper looked indignant, although he cursed the town himself for running off the cattle trade. "Now if Plainsville's as bad as all that, why did you come back, Nate?"

Nathan smiled thinly and shrugged. "It's a long story, Bert. Have you got some black coffee over there in that pot?"

The saloonkeeper was annoyed with Nate Blaine. Oh, he'd heard the stories that had been circulating about Nate killing a man in New Mexico — and maybe that wasn't the only one, either. Bert wasn't sure that he liked having a man like that sitting in his saloon day after day taking hard-earned money from the squatter men. Not that he cared for squatters, but they were the only customers he had, just about.

Groaning, Bert lifted himself from his chair and tramped heavily to the end of the bar where he kept the coffee hot over a coal-oil lamp.

And there was another thing he didn't like, Bert thought as he poured the muddy liquid into two thick cups. Plainsville had got over the notion that a man had to have a gun strapped around his middle every time he stepped out of the house. Not many of his customers were heeled these days. He was afraid Nate was going to scare all his trade away.

No doubt about it, Blaine could look plenty dangerous when he wanted to, with that revolver tied down on his right thigh like a Territory gun, and the way he looked at you out of those dark eyes.

If he had his way about it, Bert would just as soon have Nate take his business someplace else.

Surratt put the crock mugs on the table and eased into the chair again. The two men sipped at the scalding coffee, thinking their own thoughts.

It's kind of a funny thing, Bert mulled, that the Sewells would keep a case like Nate Blaine in their house. It was the boy, he guessed. They'd raised the kid like one of their own, and he had heard that kids could get a grip on you if you didn't watch them, like a good horse or a hunting dog. Maybe Wirt and Beulah were afraid Nate would take the boy away if they got his back up.

Well, it was none of his business, Bert decided. As long as Nate behaved himself and didn't start any trouble, he guessed it wouldn't hurt much to have him sitting around the saloon. It wasn't likely that some tanked-up cowhand would come in on the prod, like they used to do.

Nathan Blaine riffled the cards in his strong, lean fingers. Phil Costain, the drayman, came in, and Surratt had to get up again to wait on him.

"Howdy, Blaine," Phil said from the bar.

Nathan nodded. He did not ask Costain to the table, for the drayman would only be full of questions. Since his arrival in Plainsville, Nathan had had his fill of questions, spoken and unspoken. He knew it would be smart to pack his revolver away in a saddlebag and leave it there, but he'd be damned if he would go about half undressed just because some squatters became uneasy at the sight of a gun.

One thing he had to be proud of, anyway; his son was not afraid of guns. He had been working with the boy just a few days, and already the kid could handle the Colt's as well as a lot of men Nathan could mention.

Jeff had a knack with guns and horses — and with cards, too, for that matter. Nathan smiled quietly to himself, remembering back two days when he had been showing the boy some card tricks in the Sewell parlor. Beulah Sewell had caught him at it, and you'd have thought that Satan himself had put an evil spell on the kid, from the way she had taken on . . .

"What time is it, Bert?" Nathan called to the saloonkeeper.

Surratt looked at the big key-wound watch that he carried in his vest pocket. "Gettin' on toward four, Nate."

Almost time for the academy to let out, Nathan thought. He blocked the deck of cards that he had been riffling, and slipped them into his shirt pocket. He paid Surratt for the coffee and walked out.

Since coming to Plainsville, Nathan had set a schedule for himself that the citizens could set their watches by. At nine in the morning he rode with Jeff to the academy, then he left the horses in the public corral and took a table in Surratt's place, where he stayed until a few minutes before four. At four o'clock Nathan took his black and Jeff's bay mare out of the corral. He walked the horses up to the head of Main Street, where the boy would meet him.

"Now look here, Nate," Wirt Sewell had told him a day or so after he had started this schedule. "Jeff's got work to do at the tin shop, and he has to do it after school. A boy can't spend all his free time riding horseback and doing as he pleases."

Nathan had fixed his dark stare on Wirt and said, "Jeff's my boy. I figure I've got a say in what he can do and what he can't."

"He's living under my roof!" Wirt said angrily.

"I can take him out from under your roof. Is that what you and Beulah want?"

Wirt Sewell had melted like wax. He had blinked in disbelief and the features of his face seemed to run together. That had been the last Nathan had heard about Jeff's working in the tin shop.

Now Nathan waited with the horses at the watering trough in front of Baxter's store. Pretty soon he saw Jeff coming toward him, up the dusty side street from the clap-board schoolhouse.

This was the moment that Nathan waited for, that first sight of his son coming to meet him. The first day or two there had been other boys with him, excited and green with envy when they saw that glossy bay that Jeff could ride whenever he felt like it. It had given Nathan a warm feeling of pleasure to see his son sitting proud as a prince on that horse while the other boys danced like excited urchins around his feet.

But the other boys had stopped coming. Sometimes the Wintworth boy would come with Jeff as far as Jed Harper's bank, but he would turn off there and head for home without giving the horse or Nathan a second glance.

Nathan Blaine was not blind; he knew what had happened. He did not know how his reputation had reached all the way to Plainsville, but he did know that it had. He could tell by the uneasy way people sidled away from him. He suspected that Beulah Sewell had started the gossip herself without a speck of evidence, but there was no way of proving it. Anyway, he didn't give a damn what these people thought about him. And neither did Jeff.

The boy was a Blaine. He didn't need anybody to lean on.

But as Nathan waited by the watering trough he thought that there was not quite the spring to the boy's step that there had been before. He looked lonesome, plodding bare-foot in the deep red dust of the street.

"You look like you had a hard day," Nathan said, grinning faintly.

"It was all right."

"Would you like to ride up to Crowder's Creek with me?"

"I don't care," Jeff said, stroking the bay's glossy neck.

At that moment Nathan could see so much of Lilie in the boy that his arms ached to reach out and hold his son hard against him. But, of course, a twelve-year-old boy would never stand for a thing like that.

At that moment Nathan had a flash of inspiration. He said, "What do you say we let the horses stand a while? I just thought of some business I have to take care of."

The boy looked completely crestfallen until his pa said gently, "You come along, Jeff. The business has to do with you."

Nathan stepped up to the plank walk and Jeff followed, puzzled. Side by side they walked along the store fronts, and they could have been the only two people in the world for all the attention they paid the curious eyes that followed them from behind plate-glass windows. Nathan stopped in front of Matt Fuller's saddle shop, which was mostly a harness shop now that squatter trade had taken over the town.

Jeff's eyes widened as his pa turned in and motioned for him to follow. They walked into a rich smell of tanned leather. On the walls of Fuller's shop there hung horse collars of all sizes, and all kinds of leather harnesses and rigging. The floor was littered with scraps of leather and wood shavings; two naked saddletrees stood on a bench, and there were boot lasts and knives and all kinds of tools for the cutting and trimming and dressing and tooling of leather.

When they walked into the shop a bell over the front door jangled and Matt Fuller came up front to see what they wanted.

"I want some boots made," Nathan said.

Matt squinted over the steel rims of his spectacles. He was a wrinkled, white-haired little man who had been up in years when he first came to Plainsville fifteen years ago. But his hands were still good and strong and he was a fine leather worker when he got hold of a job that pleased him.

"You want 'em made like the ones you're wearin'?" Matt said. When Nathan said yes, the old man took his arm and led him over to where the light was better and studied the boots carefully.

"In front," Nathan said, "I want them to come about an inch short of the knee, right where the shin bone ends. The back should be cut about an inch lower. The vamps must be made of the thinnest, most pliable leather, and the tops of your best kid."

"I ain't blind," the old man snapped. "I can see how they're made. Well, you'll have to let me measure your foot. And if you want fancy stitchin' or colored insets, that'll cost you extra."

"I guess the fixin's will be up to the boy," Nathan said quietly. "The boots are for him."

The old saddlemaker snapped his head around, peering incredulously at Nathan. "Bench-made boots? For that boy?"

Jeff could hardly believe that he had heard his pa correctly. Boots of that kind were very expensive, and he had never known a boy his age having a pair made just for him. Such extravagance would appall the citizens of Plainsville. Quality boots were made to last for years; all except the thin soles, of course, which had to be replaced from time to time.

Matt Fuller snapped, "I ain't in no mood for foolishness, mister. A boy like him would grow out of his boots in no time. Then what'll you do?"

"Then," Jeff's pa said mildly, "I'll have you make another pair." Nathan saw the glow of pleasure in his son's eyes and knew that he was doing the right thing.

Matt Fuller didn't take to this idea of spoiling a sprout of a boy with fancy footgear. It was a criminal waste of money. But, after all, he was in the business, and he went grumbling to his bench and gathered up the tools he needed for measuring and fitting.

"Make those vamps snug," Nathan said as the old man made a paper cutout to fit the instep of the boy's foot. "And the arch high," Nathan added.

The saddlemaker snorted. "He won't be able to walk from here to the bank buildin'!"

"Riding boots were never meant to walk in," Jeff's father answered.

To Jeff, it was as unreal as a dream, but better than any dream he could remember. The old man didn't slight him just because he was a boy. When Matt Fuller made a pair of boots, he made them right; and besides, Jeff's pa was right there to see that he didn't get shorted.

"Now, how about the fixin's?" Nathan asked, when the measuring was done.

"Could I have my initials stitched in red thread?"

"Absolutely," Nathan smiled. "You want some do-dad stitchin'? Say a quilted pattern, or maybe a butterfly?"

It was a temptation, but Jeff decided he would rather have them like his pa's. Soft black kid from toe to tops.

At last they got it all settled with old Matt. It would take him two weeks to get them finished, the saddlemaker said, and Jeff didn't think he could possibly stand to wait that long. Already he was impatient to feel the tight fit of soft leather on his feet, but he didn't show it any more than he had to.

But just wait till Todd Wintworth and the others saw him in a pair of real bench-made boots! They'd be sick with envy, the whole bunch!

It was an odd thing, Nathan Blaine was thinking, how the glow in a boy's eyes could melt the winter in a man's soul. He guessed that he hadn't felt so good about a thing since the day he and Lilie were married.

He never should have run off, he thought, the way he had twelve years ago. But all that was in the past. Now he was determined to give the boy the best that was in him, teach him everything he knew.

It was a month to the day since Nathan Blaine had ridden unannounced and unwelcomed into Plainsville. Beulah Sewell had just brought in an armful of wood for the cookstove, and was stacking it neatly in the woodbox when Wirt came in the kitchen door. Beulah peered out the window and saw that the sun was almost an hour high.

"You locked shop early," she accused her husband.

Wirt walked heavily across the kitchen and sat at the oilcloth-covered table. Only then did Beulah notice the bleakness of Wirt's eyes, the prominence of worry lines around his mouth.

"Oughtn't Jeff be bringing that wood in for you?" Wirt asked.

Beulah snorted. "Jeff Blaine's got too big for chores," she said bitterly. "All he thinks about is rubbing his new boots and horseback riding."

"That ain't all he thinks about," Wirt said.

That was when Beulah Sewell knew that something was wrong. She turned to her husband, brushing stovewood chips from her apron. "What do you mean, Wirt?"

He moved uncomfortably on his chair, and Beulah could see that he was beginning to wish that he had never brought it up. But she waited patiently, and at last he started: "Probably it's nothing at all." And that was the worst thing he could have said. All bad news, it seemed to Beulah, started with "probably it's nothing at all." "What I mean —" Wirt tried again — "I got to talking with Marshal Blasingame, and somehow the subject of Nathan and Jeff came up —"

"I knew it!" Beulah said. "Nathan Blaine's in some kind of terrible trouble! I knew it the minute I laid eyes on him, when he came riding up here that day as big as you please, with that rifle on his saddle. I never saw the revolver at first, may the Lord help me, or I never would have let him in my house."

"Beulah, Beulah," her husband said wearily, "it's nothing like that at all. Leastwise, if Nate's in trouble, Elec Blasingame knows nothing about it."

"Well, he ought to. There's plenty of talk!"

"But it's only talk," Wirt said patiently. "When the rail-road comes, and the telegraph, Elec will be able to track down what talk he hears, but not now. Anyway, what he was telling me is something entirely different."

"Well, don't keep me in the air!" Beulah said. "Can't you come right out and say whatever it is?"

"I'm trying, Beulah. Well, the talk got around to Nate and Jeff, like I said, and Elec mentioned that he'd been up toward Crowder's Creek and had seen them there."

"I'm not surprised," his wife said shortly. "No time for anything but horseback riding, neither of them."

"And target practice," Wirt added.

Beulah blinked and looked puzzled.

"I'm putting it just the way Elec said," Wirt told her. "He said he saw Nate and the boy there on the bank of the creek. They were shooting up just about everything in sight, according to Elec."

His wife looked indignant at such a thought. "Why, Jefferson is just a child, not much more'n a baby! He can't shoot a gun!"

"What I'm trying to tell you," Wirt went on, "is that his pa was teaching him how to shoot. They were having a regular drill, Elec said, with Nate showing the boy just how to aim and everything."

Beulah was struck dumb at such a suggestion. Her mouth worked, but she made no sound. She sank slowly onto a chair across the table from her husband.

Wirt shook his head. "I know. I couldn't believe it, either. But Marshal Blasingame is not a lying man. He swore he saw Jeff firing Nate's revolver, and doing a better job at it than most men."

Beulah Sewell's small round face was hard as concrete. "Wirt, we've got to do something."

Only once before could Wirt remember seeing that bitter look of self-righteousness on his wife's face. That memory took him back ten years or more, and in his mind he could still see the stricken face of Widow Stover just before she'd been railroaded out of town. The "widow" had been known in Plainsville as a loose woman, though few, if any, could tell exactly how the epithet had been earned. She had worked a while at the Paradise eating house, where the rougher element congregated. On top of that, the widow's cheeks appeared unnaturally pink to some, and it was rumored that she painted them. Also, the widow had an exceptionally brassy voice and loved to laugh.

Wirt Sewell could not explain just why Widow Stover came to his mind at this moment, but he thought it had something to do with that set hardness in Beulah's face. That time so long ago she had looked at him in just the same way: iron-hard wrinkles around her small, pursed mouth, her pale eyes ablaze. "Wirt," she had said that time, in just the same voice, "we've got to do something." And the next day a delegation of Plainsville women had escorted Widow Stover to the stage office, where they purchased for her a one-way ticket out of the county.

What all this had to do with Nathan Blaine, Wirt was not sure, but his wife frightened him when she looked at him this way.

Wirt cleared his throat. "I was thinking," he said uneasily, "maybe we ought to have a talk with Nate."

"It's too late for talk," his wife said stiffly.

"Now, Beulah," he tried to soothe her. Let's don't look at this thing the wrong way. Nate's the boy's father; we can't forget that. It's only natural for a father to want his son to be proud of him. So we really can't blame Nate for showing off a little in front of the boy."

"He's teaching his son to kill!"

"Now, Beulah," Wirt said gently, "it ain't that at all. I guess guns are what Nate is best at. Now Mac Butler, the blacksmith, forges the best carving knives in the whole Southwest — that's what he's proud of, and that's what his son is proud of. It's the same with Nate, except Nate takes to guns instead of knives."

"It ain't the same," his wife said flatly.

Inwardly, Wirt knew that he was doing badly and would never get his point across the way he saw it. Still, something made him keep trying.

"I know it ain't the same, exactly," he said, "but in a way it is. We ought to talk to Nate and make him see it ain't right for a boy Jeff's age to know so much about guns. We ought to get him to teach the boy something else, something he'll be able to use later in life."

"You'd be wasting your time," Beulah told him. "I know Nathan Blaine. He's a wild one and always has been. I warned Lilie against him, but she wouldn't listen to me. There's only one thing to do. We've got to separate Jefferson from his pa, and the sooner we get about it, the better!"

Her husband looked worried. "Beulah, what have you got in mind to do?"

"I don't know yet. Maybe we'll just have to wait for something. Meanwhile, we can be giving it some thought."

She said no more. Her eyes burning a bit brighter, her back a bit stiffer, she went on about her work.

CHAPTER FIVE

Jeff Blaine could hardly believe that six months ago he had been a barefoot boy that people never gave a second glance to. Now he was "young Blaine," well past his thirteenth birthday and in his last year at the academy. When he crossed the street, people looked at him and said, "There goes young Blaine. Nate Blaine's boy."

It was a strange feeling, waking up after twelve years and having people look at you for the first time. It was almost as though he had been invisible before.

Jeff liked the feeling that went with being visible. It gave a person a sense of importance to see heads turn when you walked past. He liked to watch mouths moving and know that they were talking about him. It didn't make much difference what they said. The knowledge that they were talking about him was the important thing.

His life had become a bit more complicated than it had been before, but Jeff didn't mind. If the boys at the academy wanted to be jealous of him, let them. He didn't need them. And if parents told their boys to steer clear of Jeff Blaine, that was all right too.

There was just one thing that bothered him. That was Amy Wintworth . . .

Jeff still remembered that birthday party of hers that should have been such a success, and wasn't. The party had been pretty much like a dozen others that Jeff had attended, with hand-turned ice cream, and cake, and paper napkins. No matter how hard Amy and Mrs. Wintworth tried to mix them up, the boys soon separated from the girls, starting their own strictly male game of one-and-over.

For the first time in his life Jeff felt out of place and uncomfortable. He felt superior to one-and-over, so he stood apart from the others, trying to be cool and aloof.

"This is terrible!" Amy told him. "Jeff, can't you get the boys to mix with the girls?"

And he had thrown back his head, exactly like Nathan Blaine. "I can't stop them from being kids all their lives, if that's what they want."

"Well, won't you come over and talk to us?"

He had been outraged at this suggestion. "No, I can't," he said, drawing himself up. And so he had cut himself away from the others and was left standing, one small island, between the two groups. He was lonely and angry in his chosen position of isolation, but he lounged against one of the clothesline posts, yawning with elaborate casualness to hide his feelings.

"Stuck up!" he heard Lela Costain hiss acidly.

And several of the girls gathered in a small cluster and Jeff knew they were talking about him. Amy and Mrs. Wintworth had still tried to draw the two groups together, but by then the girls were as interested in their sharp, pointed gossip as the boys were in their one-and-over. Amy pointedly ignored Jeff, and he knew that she was angry.

Well, he thought, she'd get over it. Just the same she had never been prettier than she was that night, and Jeff kept glancing at her when he thought she wasn't looking.

He wished that she would come over and talk to him again, but she was too proud for that.

Probably every party reaches a point where it seems to be falling to pieces, and that was the way it was then, on Amy's eleventh birthday. But you'd never know it to look at Amy. She carried herself straight and proud, and her bright smile seemed as permanent as a steel etching. Nothing could erase it.

And yet the smile vanished when she approached the group of girls. A grimness appeared at the corners of her mouth when she heard what they were saying. Her chin jutted with determination.

"That's enough," Amy said quietly. There was a brittleness in her voice, an urgency, that made the girls look around.

"I was just saying —" Lela Costain started.

"I heard!" Amy replied coldly.

The Wintworth back yard became suddenly quiet. The boys stopped their one-and-over and began moving forward to see what was wrong.

Lela Costain, a stocky, square-built girl, shot glances around the small circle, smiling when she saw that everyone was eagerly awaiting her next word. "Well," she said primly, smoothing down her blue ruffled dress, "it's the truth. Everybody knows about Nate Blaine."

"Lela Costain, I don't want to hear another word!" Amy said sharply, and the look of self-satisfaction dropped from Lela's face. She looked flustered and ready to cry, and suddenly she turned and ran from the back yard.

That was the last they saw of Lela Costain that night.

That was all there was to it, but the entire character of the party was changed. The rowdy boys now shuffled uneasily, the girls were strangely mute. The party was as good as dead.

In Jeff's ears the sound of his father's name was still ringing. Lela had said something bad about his pa — that much was clear. He hated the thought of having a girl take up a fight that was rightly his, and yet he was proud of Amy for doing it. He couldn't very well fight a girl himself.

Within a matter of minutes the Wintworth back yard was empty. Reasons were suddenly thought of for going home early that night, and soon only Jeff and Amy were left.

"I guess," Amy said, "the party is over."

"It sure looks like it," he said awkwardly. "Well, I guess I'd better be going." But he stopped before reaching the gate. "I'm proud of you, Amy. I guess Lela Costain won't be telling lies about people after this."

"Proud of me!" He hadn't expected her sudden anger. "What happened was your fault, Jeff Blaine, not Lela's!"

"My fault?"

"How do you think the others felt, with you standing off to yourself, thinking that you were too good to mix with the rest of us? You can't do that and not get talked about!"

Jeff had never seen a girl as hard to make out as Amy. One minute she was on your side, and the next minute she was blaming him for everything. Now the fire of anger was in her eyes; he could almost feel the sparks fly as she glared at him. He felt that he had better leave as quietly as possible.

"Jeff!" He had just reached the gate when she called. Another girl would have cried her eyes out because her party had been ruined, but not Amy Wintworth. She came toward him, walking very straight. "I guess I didn't mean all the things I said, Jeff. It wasn't really your fault."

He felt awkward, and did not know what to say.

"I'll make it up with Lela tomorrow," she said. "Everything will be all right."

He knew that it had been largely his fault and he wanted to tell her so. But the words would not come. He could only stand there looking at her, and the longer he looked the prettier she seemed to get. "Well —" he said, clearing his throat — "I guess I'd better go."

For a long while that night, after going to bed, he thought over what had happened. Amy had nerve — and he had learned to appreciate nerve from his pa. Remembering how she had stepped in to take his part gave him a warm and pleasant feeling. Perhaps for the first time he actually thought of Amy Wintworth as his girl.

This thought so occupied his mind that it did not occur to him to wonder what Lela Costain had been saying about his pa. Probably he would have passed it off as nothing if it hadn't been for something that happened shortly after, at school.

Alex Jorgenson was fourteen, a straw-haired, red-faced boy who outweighed Jeff by twenty pounds. Jeff never liked him, never had much to do with him until that day when he came into the cluster of boys at the rear of the schoolhouse. Alex was talking, and the others were listening intently.

"It's a fact," Alex was saying. "My pa told me, and he says it's the gospel truth."

Jeff stood back a little from the group, assuming an attitude of cool disinterest. He wore new jeans that his pa had bought him, and his fine black boots, and he had a belt with a genuine Mexican silver buckle. A person dressed in such fine clothes could hardly afford to mix with barefoot urchins. He kept his distance.

"What did your old man say?" one of the boys asked Alex Jorgenson.

"Well, he got it straight from the traveler," Alex said. "This traveler'd been up in New Mexico Territory, so he knew what he was talking about."

"What was the story?" someone asked impatiently.

"Hold your horses, will you?" Alex said, loving the attention, wanting to draw it out as long as possible. "I'm tellin' you about the traveler so you'll know the story's straight and I'm not making it up. This traveler's horse'd thrown a shoe, and he'd stopped at Butler's to get it fixed up — that's where my pa works."

"We know your pa works for Mac Butler," Todd Wintworth said. "But what has it got to do with Blaine?"

Jeff felt his scalp tingle at the mention of his father's name. He was afraid that they were going to look around and see him standing there — but they didn't.

"This is the way it happened," Alex said confidentially, dropping his voice so that Jeff could barely hear him. "This traveler claimed he'd been in this town, a place called Limerock, up in the New Mexican country. When the name of Nate Blaine turned up in the talk, my pa said this stranger turned green around the gills and said he wouldn't stay overnight in a town where Nathan Blaine lived."

"Why not?" Todd Wintworth put in again.

"Because Blaine killed a man in Limerock!" Alex said, pausing a moment for dramatic effect. "The traveler swore it was the gospel truth; he was there. Shot this man dead, Nate Blaine did, in a poker game. The stranger said they were still looking for him over New Mexico way."

For one long moment Jeff stood still as stone.

"I've heard that story before," one of the boys said.

"But not from a man that was actually there!" another one said.

"That's what I'm telling you!" Alex said importantly. "This is the truth; you've got to believe it." Then he drew himself up, scowling. "Unless somebody wants to call me a liar."

Alex was a good deal bigger than the others. "Wait a minute, Alex. Nobody said you was a liar."

"Well, they better not!"

Jeff spoke. "And what if they do?"

All heads snapped in Jeff's direction. They saw him then for the first time, and some of them looked worried.

Jeff hardly recognized the voice that came from his throat. He stood so stiff and straight that his back began to ache. A cold fury raged within him.

He said, "I call you a liar, Alex. I call you a double damn liar."

Alex Jorgenson looked startled.

"Do you admit you're a liar?" Jeff demanded.

Alex sneered. He was heavier and older, but he wasn't sure that he liked what he saw in Jeff's eyes.

"Admit it!" Jeff said hoarsely.

"Are you crazy?" Alex tried to laugh.

"You admit it, or you'll be sorry."

Alex tried to blow himself up. He glanced at the others, drew in a deep breath and swaggered forward. "Just what do you think you're going to do about it? You want to fight, that's fine with me!"

"Gentlemen don't fight with their fists."

The words surprised Jeff almost as much as they did Alex and the others. Then he remembered that he had heard his father say it several times in describing men like Longley and Hardin.

The shadow of worry vanished from Alex Jorgenson's eyes. He laughed. "You're yellow, Jeff Blaine! You're afraid to fight."

"You admit you're a liar," Jeff repeated grimly.

"And what if I don't?"

"I'll kill you."

Alex did not hear the danger in the words. He laughed once more. "You're yellow!" he said again, and then he lunged at Jeff, hitting him solidly in the face with his big right fist.

Jeff reeled back under the impact, stumbled and fell to the ground. Anger was hot within him. He lost sight of Alex's advantage in age and weight. He was ready to shove himself up and fly into the grinning red face that leered down at him. Then, in his mind, he heard his father saying: "Gentlemen don't fight with their fists." He stayed down.

Alex Jorgenson was pleased and surprised with his easy victory. He looked at the others, grinning.

"What did I tell you? He's yellow!"

Todd Wintworth was the only one among them to see the danger. He stepped forward, shoving at Alex. "Get away from here, fast! Before somebody gets hurt!"

Alex pushed him away. He strutted now, savoring the situation. "Nobody's going to get hurt," he bragged. "Jeff Blaine's too yellow to get up and take his beating."

Jeff spoke hoarsely from the ground. "We'll see who's yellow, Alex! I'll meet you at the cottonwood grove on Crowder's Creek when school gets out. And you'd better bring a gun!"

Jeff would not soon forget the look on Alex Jorgenson's face as the blood drained from it.

Jeff picked himself off the ground and carefully brushed the dust from his new jeans. "I know your pa's got a forty-five," he said coldly. "It won't be any trouble to snitch it." He allowed himself a thin smile, not realizing how much he resembled his father at that moment. "I'll see you at the creek," he said. "Unless you're yellow, Alex." Then he turned and walked away.

That day, sitting there at his plank bench in the crowded schoolhouse, Jeff could feel the shocked and frightened stares of the pupils upon him. But he didn't care what they thought of him.

He was young Blaine, the son of Nate Blaine. From time to time he would look around to see how Alex Jorgenson was taking it. The boy was still pale. Alex was scared half to death and everybody in the room knew it.

He'll never meet me at the creek, Jeff thought with a sneer. He's yellow clear through.

But Jeff was wrong. At the end of the day Alex and several other boys came up to him in the schoolyard.

Jeff said, "You backing down?"

Alex swallowed. "No. It'll take a little time to get my pa's gun. But I'll be there."

Jeff would have sworn that Alex never would have gone through with it. But there was a saying that cornered rats would fight, and maybe that accounted for it. Jeff tried not to show his surprise. "Well, just see you don't take too long. I can't wait all day."

He turned and walked off from the others. Todd Wintworth ran across the yard to catch up with him.

"You're not really going through with it, are you, Jeff?"

Jeff almost laughed. Todd's eyes were popping. "I'm going through with it, all right. I'll teach him to go around telling lies about the Blaines."

"Are you sure it's lies?"

Jeff stopped in his tracks. "What do you mean by that?"

Todd Wintworth was no coward. He had fought plenty of boys bigger than himself and usually came out on top. But there was something about the set of Jeff's mouth that made him back water.

"I didn't mean anything."

Jeff stepped out again, walking on hard ground when he could, to keep the red dust from settling on his boots.

"Jeff," Todd said, "will you tell me something?"

"Sure."

"Are we friends, or not? You've been acting so funny lately —"

Jeff looked at him. "Sure we're friends. We've always been friends, haven't we?"

"Will you do something for me?" Todd asked.

"What?"

"Go after Alex and tell him not to get the gun."

Jeff turned on him. "Are you crazy?"

"Go after him, Jeff, before it's too late!" His voice had a curious twang to it, like a fiddle string about to snap. "Fight him with your fists. I know you're not afraid of him. He's mostly blubber and you can whip him easy."

"I don't want to whip him with my fists," Jeff said grimly. He started walking again, and this time Todd stood where he was, letting Jeff go on alone.

Well, to hell with him! Jeff told himself. I don't need Todd Wintworth or anybody else!

Today he did not take the street that went past Jed Harper's bank building, because he knew his pa would be waiting there for him. He cut up the wide alley behind Baxter's store, circled in front of the public corral and headed toward the Sewell house. He was careful not to go past the tin shop and not to let Aunt Beulah see him when he got home.

When he was sure that nobody was watching, Jeff headed for the cowshed where Nathan had hung his saddlebags from a rafter. He knew that his pa kept an extra .45 and several boxes of cartridges in one of the bags.

Sure enough, when he got the leather pouches down he found a heavy Colt's Cavalry carefully wrapped in oiled rags. He loaded it with five rounds from the ammunition carton, easing the hammer down on the empty chamber. He carefully wiped the oil from the revolver and then hid it away inside his shirt.

He felt his heart hammering with excitement, but he was not nervous or scared. His hands were perfectly steady. He peered around the shed wall to make sure Aunt Beulah hadn't seen him, and then he darted around the front of the house and headed toward Harkey's pasture. If anybody wanted to know, he was just heading to the pasture to fetch Bessie.

But nobody wanted to know.

When he reached the barbed-wire gate, he turned north and followed the fence toward Crowder's Creek. When he was sure no one could see him, he took out the revolver and tried to hold it the way his pa did.

His hands were large for a boy of thirteen, but not large enough to handle a gun as big and heavy as a Colt's .45. He could cock it with his thumb, but it was a strain and took some time. It would be better, he decided, to cock with the left hand and trigger with the right, a technique known as fanning.

Nathan Blaine did not like fanning as a technique for rapid shooting. There were only two excuses for using it: one was when you were standing belly to belly with the man you were shooting at, and the other was when your hand wasn't big enough to cock with the thumb on recoil, in the accepted fashion.

Jeff's hand simply wasn't big enough, so he would have to fan.

Not that it bothered him. His pa had taught him more about guns than most people learn in a lifetime.

As he neared the creek, Jeff practiced rolling the gun in his right hand. But two and a quarter pounds, plus the added weight of the ammunition, was a lot of weight to spin on one finger, even for a man. Jeff stopped it and was carrying the revolver at his side when he arrived at the grove of cottonwoods.

Bud Slater and Rob Lustrum, two boys from the academy, were already there. Jeff scowled as he saw them.

"Did anybody see you coming this way?"

"No," Bud Slater said. "We come up the path as if we was goin' to the pasture. Gee, is that a real Colt's?"

"Sure. What did you think it was?" He enjoyed watching their eyes grow wider.

"Do you think Alex'll show up?" Rob Lustrum wanted to know.

"Maybe. If he doesn't lose his guts," Jeff said. He spun the revolver once for their benefit. Then his trigger finger began to weaken from the weight and he shoved the revolver into his waistband.

"Is that your pa's gun?" Bud asked in awe.

But Jeff was here on serious business; he had no time for talking. He walked off to the crest of the rise, and looked down toward the town. He could see no one.

Alex wasn't going to show up. He had known it all along. Well, he'd wait a while longer. He didn't much care whether Alex showed up or not. He wanted to feel the Colt's in his hand but he was afraid his arm would get tired, and that was a chance he couldn't take. A person couldn't hit anything if his arm was weak and shaking.

After fifteen minutes had passed, Rob Lustrum said, "Looks like nobody else is coming."

"I'm not surprised," Jeff said coolly. "I didn't think Alex Jorgenson had all the guts he brags about."

"Wait a minute," Rob said, jogging up the ridge. "I think I see somebody. Yes sir, he's headin' this way, all right. But it ain't Alex."

Jeff walked back down to the cottonwoods. He would wait another fifteen minutes, he thought, and then to hell with Alex Jorgenson.

"It looks like a man," Rob said from the ridge.

"Come on down from there," Jeff said shortly. "We don't want to cause a commotion. If it ain't Alex, then it makes no difference who it is."

Rob came down from the ridge and the three boys squatted under the trees. A few minutes passed and the silence became uneasy. "Maybe I'd better go up and have another look," Bud Slater said.

Jeff just looked at him and Bud made no move toward the ridge. Then they heard somebody crashing through the undergrowth along the creek bank.

"Where are you?" a voice yelled hoarsely. "Damn it, where are you?"

Bud and Rob looked at each other and then at Jeff. It was a man's voice, and it sounded mean. Then a tall, angry figure broke into the clear and stood on the ridge for a moment in an angry crouch. It was Feyor Jorgenson, Alex's old man.

Bud Slater and Rob Lustrum jumped to their feet as if to run, and then they stood frozen as old Feyor came tramping savagely down the slope in their direction.

Jeff saw at a glance what had happened. Either Alex had gone yellow and blurted the whole story to his pa, or old Feyor had caught him sneaking his pistol and had beat the truth out of him. It didn't matter which. Jeff saw that he was in a spot.

Old man Jorgenson's temper was legend in Plainsville, but Jeff had never seen him quite as mad as he was now. His small bloodshot eyes seemed to be spurting fire from beneath his shaggy brows. His heavy blacksmith's shoulders were hunched like some big cat ready to spring, the hard muscles standing out like knotted rope beneath his sweat-stained hickory shirt. Feyor raked Bud and Rob with one savage look and then ignored them. To Jeff he snarled, "You're that damn outlaw's kid, ain't you?"

Jeff felt something go hard inside him. He stood slowly, wondering if he could draw and trigger the Colt's before old Feyor could spring.

"My name is Jefferson Blaine," Jeff said clearly.

He did not think it strange that a mere boy should stand there coolly, facing up to an ox of a man like Feyor Jorgenson. Jeff carried the difference in his waistband. Let old Feyor start something, if he wanted to. Just let him start it.

"You no-account young whelp!" Jorgenson shouted. "You want to fight, do you? You want to fight with guns, do you? Well, by hell, I'm goin' to teach you there's somethin' more dangerous than guns! I aim to give you the whallopin' of your life!"

Within Jeff's rigid frame a fuse was burning. Not yet, he thought coldly. Not yet . . . Wait for him to come at me. He's almost ready. The fuse is burning short. Now!

Old Feyor sprang at him.

Jeff grabbed the Colt's from his waistband, cocked it hard with the heel of his left hand and triggered with his right. The explosion was like thunder, but the shot was wild, and Jorgenson did not stop. The bulk of him loomed like a thunderhead and he came down on Jeff like a mountain.

An enormous fist lashed out, and Jeff's pistol flew from his hand. Feyor cuffed with his other hand, like a grizzly ripping out a deer's belly, and the world spun.

Jeff struck the ground with the side of his face. His head rang. He fell head over heels and couldn't seem to stop rolling. There was no breath in his lungs.

Old Feyor stood over him, cursing like a madman. He grabbed the front of Jeff's shirt and jerked him to his feet. Jeff saw the huge openhanded fist loom in his face and explode again. He went spinning, tumbling, falling in the other direction.

He was helpless. There was thundering pain in his head and a razor in his side. And every time he hit the ground, old Feyor would grab him to his feet, the open fist looming up again.

Through it all he could hear Feyor cursing. "You try to kill my boy! You are evil! You are like your pa, an outlaw! A killer! I teach you! Pull a gun on Feyor Jorgenson, will you!"

How long it lasted Jeff could not say. The awful shocks of Feyor's powerful slapping became unbearable. He tried to run but Feyor caught him. He tried to scramble down the creek bank, but Feyor jerked him up and slapped him again. Shamelessly, Jeff wanted to cry, but there was no breath in his lungs for crying. He wanted to beg for mercy but could not speak.

Suddenly it stopped.

Jeff lay on the ground, his head throbbing, his mouth salty with blood. A pair of strong hands took his shoulders and turned him over.

"You all right, son?"

It was Nathan Blaine, his pa.

Jeff opened his eyes and saw others coming down the slope to the cottonwoods. Phil Costain, Mac Butler, old

Seth Lewellen, Elec Blasingame, and several others. Marshal Blasingame and Mac Butler were holding Feyor by his arms and Feyor was still cursing.

"Jeff, are you all right?" Nathan asked again, anxiously.

Jeff nodded. He tried moving his legs and arms and they seemed to be all right. His pa took a red handkerchief from his back pocket and wiped some of the blood and dirt from Jeff's face. Nathan helped his son to sit up and he said, "You'll be all right when you get your breath."

The voice was gentle, but Jeff had never seen a fire so bright as the one that showed in his pa's eyes. Nathan said, "Just sit where you are. I'll take you down to the Sewells' in a minute."

Nathan Blaine rose to his feet, taller by inches than any man present. His head thrown back, he glared his hate at Feyor Jorgenson. The other men seemed uneasy, not knowing exactly what to do.

"Jorgenson," Nathan said, his voice as cold and brittle as winter ice, "I never want to see your face again. Do you understand?"

Marshal Blasingame said, "Just a minute, Nate."

"I mean it, Jorgenson," Nathan added. "If I ever see your face in Plainsville again . . ." He left the words hanging, the frosty silence more expressive than anything he could say.

Elec Blasingame's face was flushed. "You hold your tongue, Nate!" he said sharply. "And for you, Jorgenson, I'm not standing for what you did to this boy, no matter what cause you might have had. You'll likely get your day in court for this, but it'll be square and legal."

Nathan said nothing, but twin seas of rage were in his eyes, a silent warning to Jorgenson. Elec said shortly, "Nate, you'd better take the boy home."

Nathan stood like stone, making his warning absolutely clear. Jorgenson squirmed as these fierce eyes fixed themselves upon him. He looked down at the ground, his face slightly gray.

Blasingame shot an angry glance at Nathan, then turned to Feyor. "Get this straight, Jorgenson; you don't have to be afraid of anybody but the law."

But Jorgenson did not look up or indicate in any way that he had heard. Nathan Blaine's deadly warning had reached him, sapping his anger and his strength. Feyor was a strong, proud man, and he had no wish to die. He said emptily, "I guess I better get back to my work." Restraining hands fell from his arms, and he turned and tramped heavily up the grade.

The marshal glared his anger at Nathan, but he knew there was nothing he could do unless a more tangible form of violence arose from this. He threw a hard glance around at the other men and said, "All right, it's all over. Get on back to town."

After the others had gone, Blasingame stood looking down at Jeff. "Are you all right, boy?"

Jeff nodded and rose stiffly to his feet. The marshal said abruptly, "Take him home, Nate. Then I want to see you in my office."

Nathan gave him a short nod as if to say maybe he'd come and maybe he wouldn't. Red in the face, Blasingame left them.

There was a strange gray look around the edges of his pa's lips, Jeff noticed, as Nathan picked his spare Colt's out of the grass and put it into his back pocket. He did not mention the gun at all, nor the fact that Jeff had taken it from the saddlebag. All he said was: "I left my black down the creek a piece. We can ride double to town."

They had hardly more than reached the cowshed when Beulah flew into them. Jeff had never heard such carrying on. She was red in the face and her eyes popped, and that tight little mouth of hers spewed the meanest things Jeff had ever heard — even for Aunt Beulah.

The way she pitched into them, you'd get the idea that Jeff had been at fault all the way and Feyor Jorgenson was as white as snow. And it beat Jeff why his pa took everything she had to say and didn't come back with a word of his own. Aunt Beulah was going at it so hard that Jeff didn't have time to wonder how the news had got around so fast. It seemed as if the whole town knew about it.

When his aunt started accusing Nathan of being a murderer and of teaching his son to kill, Jeff started to pitch in with a piece of his own. But his pa squeezed his shoulder with a hard, lean hand, and Jeff shut his mouth without saying a word.

The same thing happened when Aunt Beulah told his pa that he was a disgrace to the family and she didn't want him in her house any more.

Jeff was going to tell her that he wasn't going to stay either if his pa couldn't. But that strong hand on his shoulder silenced him.

Then Nathan said, "All right, Beulah, that's enough."

There was something in the quiet way he said it that made Aunt Beulah pull up short. She scowled, her round little mouth as hard as a knothole in an oaken plank.

Nathan said, "I'll get out of your house, Beulah. You don't have to say any more."

Jeff pulled himself up as tall as possible, filled with anger. "I'll go, too!"

"No," Nathan said quietly. "Not now. I'll tell you when."

Beulah looked as though she had been slapped, but Nathan did not look at her again. Jeff wanted to argue, but he watched his pa turn and walk ramrod-straight to the cowshed, and decided against it.

Nathan got his saddlebags from the shed. He walked stiffly to the kitchen and got his roll. The saddlebags slung across his shoulders, the roll under his arm, Nathan walked over to his son.

"I'll put up in town someplace," he said. "Jeff, you stay here and mind your aunt and uncle."

Jeff's mouth flew open to protest, but his pa said sternly, "This ain't the right time for palaver. You do as I say." He put one strong hand on the boy's head and shook him gently. "I'll be seein' you." He swung up to the saddle and rode out of the yard.

CHAPTER SIX

The next day Jeff began to feel the new status that he had achieved in Plainsville. He was heading for the academy that morning and ran across Bud Slater near the public corral.

"Did I catch the dickens when I got home last night!" Bud said proudly. "My old man was mad as hops when he found out I'd gone to the creek without tellin' him anything about the fight."

Jeff nodded, but said nothing. Although they were nearly the same age, Jeff felt much older than he had a few days ago.

"I'll bet your aunt raised the roof," Bud said hopefully.

"With me?" Jeff asked coolly, implying that his aunt wouldn't dare.

"Well, Beulah Sewell's got a temper. Anybody in town will tell you that."

Jeff let it slide, suggesting that he had more important matters on his mind.

"Say," Bud said, holding the best for the last, "did you hear Alex Jorgenson and his old man lit out of town last night?"

This was news to Jeff, and he didn't try to hide it. "They did? When?"

"In the middle of the night some time; nobody knows for sure. Sam Baxter's raisin' ned, they say. Old Feyor pulled out owin' him thirty-four dollars at the store."

Jeff felt himself smiling, felt himself growing big inside. It was a strong, good feeling. Big, tough, hard-drinking Feyor Jorgenson pulling up stakes and leaving town in the middle of the night, just because Jeff's pa warned him he'd better! Jeff had known all along that his pa was a powerful man, but he hadn't been sure that he was this powerful.

The excitement of the thought made him want to laugh. Think what it meant having a father who could do things like that! No wonder all the other boys in Plainsville were jealous.

A change came over Bud's face when the two boys turned the corner at the Masonic Temple. "Say, I thought of something," Bud said. "See you later, maybe." He wheeled and hurried across the street, hands in pockets, elaborately casual.

That was a strange thing for him to do, Jeff thought, for Bud was heading for the schoolhouse, the same as Jeff was. But the reason for Bud's abrupt action was soon clear. Forrest Slater, Bud's old man, was coming toward him from the other end of the street.

It gave Jeff a queer feeling for a minute when he realized that Bud was afraid to be seen with him. But that hard core of bigness kept him from showing it. He looked old man Slater right in the eye as they passed.

A short way past the temple building Jeff saw Amy Wintworth come out of her house and head toward the academy. He quickened his step along the dirt path, coming up beside her. "Hello," he said.

She gave him a cool glance. "Todd's gone on ahead," she said, her chin in the air.

"I'm not lookin' for Todd."

"Oh," she said, walking on.

They walked silently. It grated Jeff's nerves that she wouldn't look at him but stared straight ahead. She didn't even notice the bruises that Jorgenson had put on his face.

There seemed no graceful way to fall back or hurry on past her, so he walked forward stiffly, throwing her a glance from the corner of his eye. Surely she had heard about his standing up to Alex Jorgenson, something not many boys his age and size would have done.

At last he felt that the silnece had lasted long enough.

"My pa was busy this morning," he said. "That's why I'm walking instead of riding the bay."

All he got was a sour look.

"Well, can't you say something?"

"About what?" she demanded.

He shrugged uncomfortably and thought that he never should have caught up with her. She was in a mood, all right, but it did not prepare him for what was to come. She turned on him suddenly, and her eyes glistened with indignation.

"You're right proud of yourself, aren't you?" she snapped. "You think you're something big, don't you, because your father scared a drunken old smithie out of Plainsville?"

Jeff felt the heat anger in his face. "I didn't say a thing about old man Jorgenson, or Alex either!"

"But you were thinking it!" she accused unreasonably. "Oh, I can see the smugness on your face, Jefferson Blaine!"

How could a man defend himself against an assault like that?

"And another thing," she said. "I heard my father tell Todd not to have anything to do with you or your pa. So don't go running after him."

If she were a boy, Jeff thought angrily.

But she wasn't. She was a frail girl with pink lips and flashing brown eyes and a yellow ribbon in her hair. Just the same, her words hurt. So Ford Wintworth, her pa, had forbidden Todd to have anything to do with him! And that probably went for Amy too.

Jeff looked at her, then turned suddenly in anger and started to walk away.

He had taken fewer than a dozen paces when his feet began to drag. Darn it, he thought, he'd never understand girls if he lived to be a hundred. She had ruined her birthday party only to take his part — now he couldn't even get her to look at him!

Yet he consciously slowed down until she caught up with him again. "What're you mad about?" he demanded.

"I didn't say I was mad," she said coolly.

"I've got eyes. What difference does it make, anyway, what happens to Alex Jorgenson and his old man?"

"If you don't know, I can't tell you."

There seemed to be nothing else to say. Amy could use words like a lash, but they made clean wounds that healed quickly. Whatever's ailing her, Jeff thought, she'll soon get over it. They walked the rest of the way to the academy in silence.

In Elec Blasingame's office, where the county rented space in the basement of the Masonic Temple, Nathan Blaine took a chair and waited. After a minute the marshal came in from another room and said shortly, "You took your time about getting here."

"I didn't know it was urgent," Nathan said quickly.

"Old Feyor Jorgenson and his kid pulled out of town in the middle of the night; scared for their lives. That's how urgent it is."

Nathan's hand moved toward a tobacco sack in his shirt pocket. He said nothing.

Elec Blasingame was a bulldog of a man. He was squat and thick, almost completely bald. He had the enlarged, blue-veined nose of a heavy drinker, but few had ever seen him drunk. He had been marshal of Plainsville for fourteen years, through good times and bad. There were four graves on the wrong side of the town cemetery, four dead men who had thought Blasingame was just another town marshal who would back down when the going got tough.

Elec's jaws bulged as he glared at Nathan. "Nate," he said, "we've had a quiet town here since the cow outfits shifted away from Plainsville; people have got to like it that way. Now what you've been doing the past twelve years ain't much my business; I'm just the town marshal. But if you ever bear down on your gun again, the way you did with Jorgenson, you're going to have me to contend with. Is that clear?"

Nathan held a sulphur match to his cigarette and shot the stick on the floor. "Did you see me throw down on Jorgenson?"

"You know what I mean," Blasingame said harshly. "A name followed you to Plainsville when you came back. When you use a hardcase reputation to scare a man, it's the same as pulling a pistol."

Nothing showed in Nathan's face. "I'll remember. Is that all, Elec?"

"No," Blasingame said, "it isn't." He pulled up a tilt-back chair and sat solidly behind an unfinished plank table that served as a desk. "I've been thinking about that boy of yours, Nate. Doesn't it seem to you he's a little young to be so handy with a forty-five?"

Nathan studied the top of his thin cigarette. "A man can't start too young learning to protect himself."

"Protect himself? Is that what the boy is doing?" The marshal planted his elbows on the table, shoving his blunt face at Nathan. "The way I got it, your boy challenged young Jorgenson to a pistol duel. Now that's a hell of a thing for a kid to think up all by himself!"

Grayness edged Nathan Blaine's thin lips. "Maybe he had a reason."

"What kind of reason could a kid like Jeff have to want to shoot another boy?" Blasingame demanded. Suddenly his big fist hit the table. "Damn it, Nate, I'm scared for that boy of yours, and that's God's truth!

Can't you see what you've done to him? Teaching a boy like that to use a gun is like giving a baby dynamite caps to play with!"

The fire in Nathan's eyes burned slowly. "Jeff's just a boy, like any other."

The marshal came half out of his chair. "Wes Hardin was just a boy too, once. But he'd killed a passel of men by the time he was sixteen. They say Will Bonney could cut a notch for every year of his age when he was twenty-one. Bill Longley had a price on his head when he wasn't any older than Jeff is now."

Angrily, Nathan tramped his cigarette under a boot heel. "Look here, Elec, what are you trying to say?"

Blasingame settled back, his voice suddenly gentle. "I'm just wondering what you've got on your mind, Nate. That boy looks up to you; any fool can see that. You can make out of him just about anything you want. I hope it's not a hardcase gunman."

Nathan came stiffly to his feet. "Are you through, Marshal?"

Blasingame sighed wearily and said nothing.

There was a small game going in Surratt's place when Nathan got there, but he ignored it and went to the bar. The saloonkeeper gave him a curious look when he asked for a bottle and took it to a vacant table. From the corner of his eye, Surratt watched Blaine pour a tumbler half full and down it in two choking gulps.

The raw whisky set off a blaze in Nathan's stomach but did little to chase the scare that Blasingame had given him. Damn them, why couldn't they mind their own business?

But it wasn't Blasingame so much, nor Beulah — they only helped bring this real trouble home to him. It was what Jeff had done; that was the thing that frightened him. Oh, he hadn't shown it in front of the marshal, but the knowledge that the thirteen-year-old boy had actually intended to fight a pistol duel — I'll have to talk to the boy, Nathan thought. I'll have to make him understand that guns are not to be taken lightly. Guns are meant to be used as a last resort, when everything else fails.

The chill of winter was in his belly when he thought of his son facing up to old Feyor Jorgenson, pulling a revolver on him. It's a thousand wonders, he thought, that Jeff didn't kill him. That was the worst thing that could happen to a man, Nathan knew — except to get killed himself.

Nearly half the whisky was gone now and Nathan felt limp and soured with it.

Nathan had been sitting at the table for about an hour when the drifter came into Surratt's place and had several drinks at the end of the bar. For a moment Nathan thought that he had seen the stranger before — someone he had seen in New Mexico, maybe, or down below the Big River.

Then he realized that he had never seen the man in his life. The drifters ran to type, and Nathan had seen plenty of his kind at various times, riding the high ground, living away from the law up in the Indian

Nations. That was the thing that confused him. It was the type he knew, not the man.

From habit, Nathan scanned the hitch rack outside the saloon, spotted a trail-weary dun with an expensive rig, a Winchester Model 7 snug in a soft leather boot. Nathan smiled thinly, knowing that he had pegged the man right.

The stranger was about fifty, his leathery face as sharp as a hatchet, his dirty gray hair long and shaggy. He was covered with trail grime, and was many days past needing a shave. Nathan did not know him, but he could feel that this drifter was a good man not to pick trouble with. A red handkerchief had been tamped loosely into his holster to protect his converted Frontier from dust — a precaution taken only by specialists.

After several silent minutes at the bar, the stranger counted out what he owed and walked out.

A vague uneasiness settled around Nathan after the drifter had gone.

CHAPTER SEVEN

Shortly before four o'clock that afternoon Beulah Sewell gathered up her sunbonnet and wicker basket and headed for Sam Baxter's store to buy rations for the rest of the week. On her way to the store she stopped at her husband's tin shop.

Wirt was working on a windmill, a rush order for one of the grangers, and the back of the shop was cluttered with other work that had to be put off. Beulah sniffed.

"If you ask me, it's time you put Jefferson back to work."

Her husband's mouth was a grim, thin line. "Mr. Jeff Blaine," he said sourly, "has decided he's above tin working."

"What that boy needs is a sound thrashing," Beulah snapped.

Her husband looked at her. "You're not forgetting Feyor Jorgenson so soon, are you, Beulah?"

His wife's small eyes sparked. Wirt had not dared mention Nathan Blaine's name since the affair on the creek, and now he wished that he hadn't mentioned Jorgenson's either. He changed the subject quickly.

"I've been so busy here," he said, "I haven't had a chance to get to the bank." From a cigar can he took a small packet of money and handed it to his wife. "Will you stop in at Jed Harper's and deposit that? You'll have to do it before going to Baxter's; Jed'll be locking his doors any minute now."

Beulah took the money and hid it under the napkin she had in the basket. She nodded stiffly, her jaws tight.

Wirt Sewell shook his head slowly as he watched his wife's small, prim figure move up the plank walk. He had never seen Beulah so worked up before. But maybe things would be better, now that Nathan had moved out of their house.

Jed Harper was just locking the bank's front door when Beulah reached for the big brass latch. Jed was a large, well-fed man with pink cheeks and white hair. He smiled a quick, professional smile.

"Why, hello, Beulah. I was just locking up."

"Me and Wirt managed to put by a little," Beulah said confidentially. "We wanted to bank it today, if we could."

Jed Harper's smile became a bit strained, but he stepped aside and swung the door open. "Of course, Beulah. My teller has knocked off for the day, but I can take your money and give you a receipt. Please come in."

"Thank you, Jed," Beulah said primly. She followed the banker to a railed partition where Jed eased wearily into a leather chair.

He got out pen and paper and said, "Now how much is it, Beulah? I'll just add it to your and Wirt's account."

Beulah felt the breath of the street on the back of her thin neck. She thought, Jed left the door open. Now that's a careless thing to do, with people's money in his care. But she was busy counting the money in the bottom of the wicker basket and didn't turn around. Then she heard the latch click and knew that someone had stepped through the door and closed it.

A voice said, "Stand like you are, lady. Don't turn around."

Jed Harper's eyes were bugging as though he had just caught a glimpse of the Great Beyond. "Do as he says, Beulah," the banker said hoarsely. "He's got a gun!"

Beulah stiffened. A gun meant robbery. She thought of Wirt's hard-earned money, and her small eyes glinted. No hoodlum was going to take this money, she vowed to herself; she didn't care how many guns he had.

Beulah started to wheel about. She would fight for what was hers with her own two hands, if necessary! The man behind her made a small, angry sound of surprise when he saw what she was going to do. He moved quickly, before Beulah's thought had grown to action. Beulah felt blinding pain as something hard struck the back of her head through her sunbonnet . . .

Beulah awoke in a sea of pain. Her head ached as if it would burst, and she had never known that a person could be as sick as she was that moment. The smell of oiled oak told her that she was lying on the floor of the bank. She tried to move and could not. She tried to call out, but the effort of drawing up a bare whisper brought the blaze of pain to her head.

Her money! Had the thief taken her money? She saw the blurred shape of her shopping basket turned upside down on the floor, but she couldn't reach it. She had the shameful, disgusting feeling that she was going to be sick there on the bank floor.

For a moment she slipped into a dense mist of pain. What was the matter with that Jed Harper? Why didn't he help her? Why did he leave her lying on the floor like this, helpless?

She didn't dare move her head. Every move she made caused the floor to lurch sickeningly and increased the agony in her head.

Through the mist she heard a voice snarling angrily, "I said open that vault! And be quick about it!"

Beulah heard Jed Harper's voice, sputtering and scared. A fine man he is, Beulah thought, for people to leave money with! She'd tell Wirt about this! They'd take their money out of this bank and put it somewhere else!

Still, she was afraid to move. When she opened her eyes the lurching of the room made her violently sick, and she decided to lie quietly. Sooner or later someone would come to help her. But she wouldn't depend on Jed Harper!

Then she heard boot heels running away from the vault. Beulah made herself open her eyes again, and saw a hazy, distorted form that hardly looked like a man at all. A voice shouted, "Don't try it, mister!"

A revolver exploded. The crashing sound made Beulah cringe, her eyes tightly closed. The side door of the bank opened and closed; then there was complete silence in the building.

Several seconds must have passed before realization drifted through the pain. The thief was gone. But it was so quiet . . .

Finally she realized that Jed Harper must be dead. Beulah lay like stone, her mind racing. She discovered that she could move now and the pain was not so bad. But she lay there thinking . . .

Her small, pale eyes took on the cast of steel. Every nerve in her tight-wound body twanged like a fiddle string. She made herself sit up. Her heart hammered, her head throbbed, but she forced herself not to think so much of the pain. Slowly, inch by inch, she gained her feet and stumbled to the bank's front door. She fell almost into the arms of Phil Costain.

"Miz Beulah!" the big drayman said, startled. "You better stay inside; there's shootin' goin' on somewhere!"

Beulah's throat felt raw. "Get Elec Blasingame," she said. "Get him here quick!"

Other men were gathering around. Some were running up the street trying to find out where the shot had come from. "Miz Beulah," Phil said, "you better sit down; you don't look so good to me."

"You fool!" she told him angrily, "get me the marshal! I think Jed Harper's just been killed!"

It didn't take Blasingame long to get there. His face was redder than usual, and the smell of whisky on his breath was enough to make Beulah reel. She said, "Did you get him?"

"Not yet, but we will. Did you see him, ma'am?"

Beulah locked her jaws for a moment. Then she snapped, "Aren't you going to take a look at Mr. Harper?"

The marshal turned on Bert Surratt, who had just come up. "Bert, see if you can locate Doc Shipley. Mrs. Sewell, you'd better come back into the bank and sit down."

Beulah followed Elec Blasingame into the building and sank weakly into a chair by the rail partition. Elec went to the other side of the partition, stayed a moment and came back. "Jed caught it just over the heart: never knew what hit him."

The throbbing in Beulah's head got worse. She tried to think. The most important thoughts she'd ever had were now swimming in her brain, but it was hard to keep them straight in all that pain.

"Mrs. Sewell," the marshal said, "did you get a look at this killer, the one that shot Harper?"

Beulah's thin lips compressed, her small mouth almost disappeared. She looked hard at Elec Blasingame. "Marshal," she snapped, "don't you think you ought to be out looking for the killer instead of pestering a poor hurt woman like me?"

"I just want to know if you saw the killer, ma'am." He waited a moment, then added, "There are plenty of men scouring the town, but it would help if we knew who to look for." Beulah Sewell's jaws locked again. It gave Elec Blasingame a chill to see her sitting there as cold as a block of stone. "Please, Mrs. Sewell," he said with great patience, "this is important. You are the only one alive who could have seen him."

Still, Beulah said nothing. A glassiness appeared in her pale eyes. She sat staring . . . staring . . . Elec had the chilly feeling that she was looking right through him at something on the other side of the world. Anger and impatience swelled within him.

"Look," he said shortly. "Every minute counts, ma'am. Surely you can understand that. Now please, as quick as you can, tell me exactly what happened."

Wirt Sewell burst through the front door at that moment, pale and frightened. "Beulah, you're all right!"

"My head hurts," his wife said peevishly.

Elec Blasingame, outwardly, remained calm. "Wirt, Doc Shipley'll be here directly to look her over. Now it's important that she tell us what she saw."

"Even if she's hurt?" Wirt demanded.

"Even if she's hurt!" Elec said.

After a tense moment, Beulah said, "All right, I guess I'd have to tell sooner or later, anyway."

"You don't have to talk if you don't feel like it," her husband told her.

"Damn it, Wirt!" the marshal exploded. "You stay out of this!"

By this time a good-sized crowd had gathered in the bank building, tensely waiting for what Beulah Sewell had to say. "My head hurts," she said weakly. "It must have been a gun he hit me with."

"Who hit you?" Elec put in quickly.

"I'll have to tell it my own way, Marshal. You see, Jed was locking up when I got to the bank. He let me in and was about to make me a receipt when the door opened again and in came this —"

"What did he look like?"

"He told me not to turn around," Beulah went on, as though she hadn't heard the question. "But I did. He didn't want me to look at his face; that's why he hit me. It didn't do him any good," she added grimly. "I got a good look at him. I stared right to the bottom of his mean eyes before he hit me. I guess he thought he'd killed me. He wouldn't have run off the way he did if he'd known I was alive to tell about him."

The marshal sensed that she had reached the end. "Mrs. Sewell," he said gently, "who was it?"

"May the good Lord help him," Beulah said grimly. "It was my own brother-in-law, Nathan Blaine."

CHAPTER EIGHT

A sound of amazement rose inside the building. Elec Blasingame had been prepared for almost anything — but not this. When he spoke, his voice held the rasp of urgency. "Mrs. Sewell, are you absolutely certain?"

"Of course I'm certain. I looked right at him."

"You also told me that it must have been a gun that he hit you with," Blasingame shot at her. "Seems to me that you'd have known it was a gun if you were looking at him."

Beulah's small eyes bored into the marshal's face. "You're not calling me a liar, are you, Elec Blasingame?"

"You know better than that, ma'am. I just wonder if you actually turned and looked at this man, or if you merely thought you did. Put a person's mind under a strain and it sometimes plays funny tricks."

The look she gave him chilled the marshal like a cutting rain. "My mind wasn't playing tricks!" she bit out. "I turned and looked at Nathan Blaine, and that's why he tried to kill me." She raked the crowd with her anger. "You think I wouldn't recognize my own brother-in-law? You think I like dragging my family's name in the mud? And the boy Wirt and I raised like our own — do you think I'd hurt him like this if I didn't have to?"

"All right, ma'am," Elec said heavily. "I just wanted to make sure." He turned to Bert Surratt, who was standing at his elbow. "Nate Blaine couldn't have been in your place while the bank was being robbed, could he?"

Bert shook his head. "Funny thing. Blaine started drinkin' the minute he come in from your office. He left the saloon before the shootin'. Said he needed some air."

Elec watched Beulah's face carefully, but it was set like iron and told him nothing. He turned shortly and headed for the door. "It looks like Nate Blaine's our man."

As soon as school let out Jeff headed for the bank corner where Nathan usually waited for him. His pa wasn't there today. Instead, there was a scattering crowd of angry-eyed men, most of them carrying shotguns or rifles. There was a hoarse yell from the far end of the street, near the public corral, and old Seth Lewellen came hobbling out of the bank building and said, "By golly, it sounds like they found him!"

Not since the cattle trade had quit Plainsville had Jeff seen so much excitement in the town. He pushed up to the door of the bank, trying to see what was going on. He almost ran into his Uncle Wirt and Aunt Beulah, who were just coming out.

"Jeff," Wirt said roughly, "what are you doing here?"

"The academy just let out," Jeff said, puzzled. "I always come this way. What's all the excitement about?"

"Never mind that," Wirt said. "Help me get your Aunt Beulah home; she's had an accident."

"What kind of an accident?"

Wirt looked at him, and Jeff had never seen such fire in those usually mild eyes. "Stop asking questions," he said shortly, "and take your aunt's arm."

Aunt Beulah looked kind of funny too, Jeff was thinking. She was leaning on her husband, her eyes almost closed, her face as pale and bloodless as bone china. She hardly even looked at Jeff as he got on her left side and took her arm.

"I want to go home," she almost whimpered.

"It's all right, Beulah," Wirt said gently. "Do you feel like walkin'?"

"I guess so."

"I can hustle down to the corral and rent a hack of some kind."

"No," Beulah said weakly, "I can walk all right. Don't joggle me like that, Jefferson; it hurts my head."

Jeff held her steady by the elbow. "What happened, Uncle Wirt?" he asked again, bursting with curiosity.

His uncle's voice turned harsh. "Never you mind!"

Together, they helped Beulah down the steps and began moving slowly along the walk. Jeff kept looking back at the gathering crowd at the far end of the street. It was growing larger and had a mean, rough sound to it. There was something in that sound that started a chill at the base of Jeff's spine.

They crossed the street, took short cuts toward home, and finally got Beulah to the house. Wirt made his wife lie down on the couch in the small parlor and sent Jeff to draw a bucket of cold water from the well. Wirt dipped a towel in the water and wrapped it around Beulah's head.

"How does that feel?" Wirt wanted to know.

There was a strange emptiness in her eyes. "I'm all right," she said lifelessly.

"I think I ought to see what's happened," Wirt said. "Jeff will be here if you want anything."

Jeff wanted to cry out in protest. He was crawling with curiosity and nobody would tell him anything. But he couldn't miss the urgency in his uncle's voice when Wirt turned to him and said, "You watch after her, Jeff. I won't be long. If anything comes up, you hightail it after Doc Shipley, understand?"

Reluctantly, Jeff nodded. But how could he be expected to do anything when he didn't even know what was wrong with his aunt? After Wirt was gone Jeff took a chair on the other side of the room and began his uneasy vigil. Aunt Beulah didn't do a thing but stare up at the ceiling.

This wasn't at all like his aunt; there was something about the way she lay there, motionless as a corpse, that gave him a spooky feeling. Soon he looked away and tried to fix his mind on something else.

After a long while Beulah turned her head to look at him. "Jefferson," she said weakly, "no matter what happens, I want you to remember something. I love you like you was my own son. I love you more than anything in the world, I guess."

Jeff squirmed uncomfortably. He didn't like this kind of talk, and it didn't sound like his aunt at all.

"Will you remember that, Jefferson?"

"Yes, ma'am," he said self-consciously.

She smiled then — the strangest, saddest smile that Jeff had ever seen. "That's good," she said. "Just so you remember." And then she went back to staring at the ceiling . . .

Almost an hour passed before his uncle returned. "Well," Wirt said heavily, "they got him."

He did not look at Beulah. He cast his gaze all about the room, everywhere but the couch on which his wife was lying. Slowly she brushed the wet towel from her head and sat up.

"Wirt, what happened?"

Her husband glanced sharply at Jeff and said, "Not now, Beulah."

Some of the old fire returned to Beulah's eyes. And when she jutted out her small chin and stared her husband down, Jeff knew that she couldn't be hurt very bad. She said, "The boy has to know some time. It might as well be now."

Wirt Sewell looked as though he had gained ten years in age. He dropped heavily to a cane-bottom chair. "It was not a pretty thing," he said flatly. "They were going after Nate with ropes. They would have strung him up if it hadn't been for Elec Blasingame."

The mention of his father's name set Jeff's heart to hammering. He wanted to leap up and demand to know what they were talking about, but he was unable to move or make a sound. It was almost as if he were frozen in one position, his throat paralyzed and dry.

His uncle turned to him and said with gentleness, "You'll have to know it, Jeff; your pa's in bad trouble. He robbed the bank and killed Jed Harper. Now they've caught him and got him locked up."

Jeff stared at his uncle through a sudden haze of anger. He heard himself shouting, "It's not true! You're lying!"

Wirt stared at the floor, his face gray.

"You're lying!" Jeff shouted again.

"Jefferson, you hush up!" Beulah said. Unsteadily, she stood up and took Jeff's shoulders in her hands. "It's true," she said shortly. "I tried to warn you that your pa was worthless and no good, but you wouldn't listen to your Aunt Beulah. Well, maybe now you'll listen!"

CHAPTER NINE

Shortly after sun-up Elec Blasingame arrived at his office in the basement of the Masonic Temple, to relieve the night deputy.

"Any trouble, Ralph?"

Ralph Striker, Elec's second in command, was dozing on his shotgun at the plank desk. Now he blinked and rubbed the back of his hand over his mouth. "Morning, Elec. No trouble to speak of. Plenty of talk, but that's about as far as it went."

"Lynching talk?"

The deputy shrugged. "I guess so, but they've cooled off by now."

"How about Nate Blaine; has he cooled off any?"

The deputy, a tall, gaunt man in his late forties, smiled faintly. "I don't know. I haven't been near him since midnight!"

"Did he talk?"

The smile widened, wearily. "He cusses anybody that comes within yellin' distance of his cage, if you can call that talking."

"I see," the marshal said heavily.

The deputy got up from the desk and racked his shot-gun on the wall. As Ralph Striker tramped out of the office, the marshal took the chair and scowled. Almost immediately he got up again, took the cell keys from his desk and headed down the corridor toward the single iron cage which was the Plainsville jail.

Nathan Blaine lay stretched out on a board bunk, one arm flung over his eyes. When he heard the rap of boot heels on stone, he snapped to a sitting position, his eyes bitter. The marshal paused at the iron-barred door.

"Nate, you ready to talk?"

Nathan stood up in his cage. "You haven't caught him?"

"Caught who?" the marshal asked.

"The man that robbed the bank and killed old man Harper." All the bitterness was in his eyes — his voice was only slightly edged with anger.

Elec rubbed his chin thoughtfully. "I figured we had the killer in jail," he said mildly. "However, I'm willing to listen to anything you've got to say, Nate."

With an iron will, Nathan clamped down on his nerves and anger. He forced himself to remain calm, knowing that his very life depended on how clearly he was able to think this thing out. He made himself look into the marshal's eyes and say, "You've got the wrong man, Elec."

"I'm listening."

"All right; this is what happened. I'm not a drinking man, but like a fool I got tanked up yesterday after leaving your office. I got to thinking about something, and the more I thought the more I drank. Around four o'clock I was feeling sick. I needed air. I walked to the end of the block, went around behind the bank building where the grangers hitch their teams, and was heading for the corral when I heard the shooting."

"Then what did you do?" the marshall asked.

"I couldn't tell where the shot came from. I wasn't thinking very straight. Anyway I started running the other way, toward the public corral. Then I realized I was going the wrong way. I stopped and turned around, and that was when I saw this drifter hightailing it out of the bank's side door."

"What drifter was that?" Blasingame put in.

"The one that was in Bert Surratt's place just a few minutes before. I saw him; one of those cool-eyed boys that you run across sometimes in the Indian Nations, about fifty years old, with long gray hair and a sharp face. He rode a good-looking dun with an expensive rig, and he had a Model Seven Winchester on his saddle. Surratt saw him; he can tell you."

The marshal's face had gone bland, showing nothing. "What happened to this drifter after you saw him come out of the bank's side door?"

Nathan shrugged. "I don't know. He must have lit out across the street. I figure the shooting must have been something he hadn't intended. When it happened, he figured he'd best lie low for a while and see if he could slip out of town in the confusion. I'd say that's just what he did. Before I could go after him, a lot of damn fools were trying to lynch me."

Blasingame continued to rub his chin thoughtfully.

"Look here," Nathan said, "you believe me, don't you?"

A long moment of silence passed. "Maybe I would, Nate, except for one thing. Beulah Sewell swears you're the one that gunwhipped her and shot Jed Harper."

Nathan had known this would come up, and he tried desperately to hold back his rage. He couldn't do it. He felt a wildness swarming over him and suddenly he grabbed the iron bars and began shaking the door like a madman.

"Damn Beulah Sewell! She wants to get me out of the way! She wants to bring up my boy like a milk-fed house-cat! That's the reason she lied about what she saw in the bank!"

"Now, Nate," Blasingame said quietly, "taking on like that won't help you."

"How would you feel about it?" Nathan shouted.

"Stop it!" Elec Blasingame's big voice blasted on the stone walls of Nathan's cage. "Listen to me, Nate. You're in a bad spot. Your own sister-in-law has identified you as the killer; what do you expect me to do about that?"

Nathan felt the life going out of him. Hopelessly, he loosened his grip on the bars.

Finally he said, "This would be almost funny if I didn't know that half the town had lynching on the brain. On the say-so of one woman you lock me up and accuse me of murder and robbery. I didn't have the bank's money on me when they got me, did I? And you can't prove that the bullet that killed Harper came from my gun."

"You had plenty time to hide that money," Blasingame said. "You had time to reload, too."

"Is that the kind of evidence you hang a man on in Plainsville?"

"The strongest evidence in the world. The testimony of a respectable eyewitness to the crime." This time Elec saw the storm coming, and he added quickly, "But I said I'd listen to you, and I have. I'll go back over the ground and find out what I can about this drifter you claim you saw. Is that fair enough?"

Before Nathan could answer, he saw Ralph Striker's lanky figure heading toward them. The marshal turned. "I thought you were going home, Ralph."

"I was, but I ran into something — the Blaine boy."

Nathan grabbed the bars. "Jeff?"

A new kind of worry crossed Elec Blasingame's face. "Hold the boy in my office, Ralph. Tell him he can see his pa as soon as I'm through talking to him." The marshal turned back to Nathan. "Nate," he said solemnly, "a few minutes from now you're going to have to make the most important decision of your whole life. Your boy is probably bewildered and hurt and doesn't know exactly what to think. He's come to you for an answer, and likely he'll believe everything you tell him. What are you going to say, Nate?"

Nathan stared at the marshal with hard eyes. "My boy will hear the truth!"

"Do you mean to tell him his aunt is trying to railroad you on a murder charge?"

"That, and plenty more!"

Blasingame rubbed his hand over his gleaming scalp. The bulldog look had gone from his face, and he looked like just another tired old man. He said quietly,

"Have you thought what it's going to do to the boy, Nate? The Sewells are the only people your son has, besides you. If you're convicted here, it'll be up to Beulah and Wirt to see the boy through the worst time of his life. They may not be the kind of people you like, but they're something, and they haven't done such a bad job with Jeff so far. Are you going to poison him with hate, turn him against the only people who might stand by him?"

Nathan Blaine stood rigid. In his anger he had not imagined that truth could be more deadly than a gun. Blasingame's line of reasoning left a taste of gall in his mouth, made him helpless.

The marshal said, "I'll check your story as far as I can, Nate. That's all I can do. What you tell your boy — I guess that will have to be left to you and your conscience." He turned abruptly, a thick, squat figure of a man, and walked back to his office.

Jeff did not know what to say when he saw his father standing there behind the thick iron bars. All through the violent and sleepless night he had thought of all the things he was going to say. No matter what happened, he had vowed to stick by his pa.

The vow had been sealed in tears of anger and in fits of rage against his Aunt Beulah. That night he had stopped being a boy and started being a man. He had not spoken to Aunt Beulah this morning; he had not even looked at her, and he would never in his life forgive her for the hateful lies that she had told about his pa.

But, in spite of all the pledges of loyalty that he had meant to voice, the words were stuck in his throat as he gazed up at those cruel, burning eyes on the other side of the bars. The lines of hate in his pa's face were as deep and hard as chiseled stone. Involuntarily, Jeff took a stumbling step backwards as Nathan grasped the bars in his two hands as though he meant to rip them apart.

"You're not in school!" Nathan accused him roughly.

Jeff swallowed. "It ain't time yet. I came here . . ."

". . . to see what a jailbird looks like?" his pa shot at him.

Jeff felt sickness working within him; his throat was choked and swollen. He said, "I wanted to tell you I don't believe in any of it! All the things people are sayin'!"

He was shocked when his pa threw his head back and laughed harshly. The stubble of beard gave Nathan's face a sunken, wolfish look. Sleeplessness had made his eyes bloodshot and mean.

"So you don't believe it, do you?" Nathan laughed again.

The chill of that underground cage breathed a stickiness of death in Jeff's face. His heart hammered. It was impossible to believe that iron bars could make such a change in a man. He saw his pa as he had never seen him before — a cruel, ruthless man, quick and mean in every move he made. Jeff felt himself shaking. He could no longer look up into those slitted, bloodshot eyes, but turned his gaze helplessly to the floor.

Nathan said harshly, "I don't need you to worry about me, boy. Nate Blaine can take care of himself!"

Now Jeff's whirling thoughts formed words and the words came blurting out. "But it isn't true, is it, what they're saying about the bank! You couldn't shoot an old man like Jed Harper!"

The look that Nathan threw at him made Jeff cringe. "Couldn't I? Maybe Harper was a fool, maybe he tried something that wasn't very smart. Anyway, what can a kid understand about such things!"

Abruptly, Nathan threw himself away from the barred door, facing the opposite wall of his cell. "You better get started for the academy," he said sharply. "I've got important things to think about."

Elec Blasingame sat like a block of granite as the boy stumbled blindly through his office and up the cement steps to the street. At last he looked at Ralph Striker, his deputy.

"I believe in giving the devil his due. I guess I didn't figure Nate Blaine had the guts for a thing like that."

Through the office door they could see Nathan stretched stiff as a corpse on his board bunk, facing the wall. It was one of those rare times when Elec Blasingame felt helpless and did not know what to do. At last he got up and said, "Go on home, Ralph. The town is mine for the day."

Most of the time the Plainsville marshal was a plodding, methodical man, and that was the way he went about his business today. A nagging seed of doubt had been planted in his mind, and he didn't like it. Elec

Blasingame wanted things as clean-cut as possible, either black or white.

His first stop that day was Bert Surratt's saloon, where he stated his problem bluntly.

"Think back, Bert, to just before the bank fracas yesterday. Do you remember a hardcase stranger buyin' a drink or so off you?"

The saloonkeeper rubbed a hairy fist across his mouth, thinking. "There was a stranger in, all right, but I wouldn't peg him as a hardcase. Oh, he was heeled, but all travelers go heeled unless they're fools. Gray-haired geezer, as I remember, about fifty. Looked harmless enough to me."

"Did you get a look at his animal or rig?"

"No," Bert said slowly. "Guess I didn't pay him much attention, Marshal. Why do you ask?"

"Was Nate Blaine in here the same time the stranger was?"

Surratt thought about it, scowling. "Sure. I remember because Nate was giving the old bird a goin' over. I figured Nate might have known him from somewhere, but they didn't speak. The stranger pulled out maybe fifteen minutes before Nate did."

Blasingame listened to the sound of hammering in the alley behind the saloon. "What's that noise?" he asked.

The saloonkeeper smiled. "Carpenters. They're buildin' Jed Harper's casket." He took a swipe at the bar with a dirty towel. "That damn Blaine; they should have strung him up the minute they caught him."

"But you wouldn't want to try it singlehanded, would you, Bert?" Blasingame turned and walked out of the saloon.

He made several stops between the saloon and the bank building. A clerk in Baxter's store claimed he caught a glimpse of the stranger riding up the street away from Bert's place. Old Matt Fuller, in the saddle shop, had seen the drifter watering his horse at the trough in front of the bank building; he had paid strict attention to the rig because of its quality workmanship, but had hardly noticed the man himself. After that, the stranger could have dissolved in thin air, for all anyone saw of him.

Just a drifter passing through. There was no telling where he was by now.

But the marshal didn't let it go at that. He went to the bank and stared at the bleak two-story brick building with cool, impersonal eyes. Aside from the Masonic Temple, it was the only brick building in town. Now it was locked tight. There was a black-bordered funeral notice on the door.

For the sake of supposing, Elec tried to reconstruct a situation as it might have been. The stranger had been seen watering his horse in front of the bank some time after he had left Surratt's which would put it close to four o'clock. Now, Blasingame reasoned, it's just possible that he was here when Jed let Beulah Sewell in the bank to deposit her money.

Stretching it a bit further, it's just possible that he could have heard Jed Harper telling Beulah that his help had gone and he was alone. Now, if this drifter had been a hardcase type, as Nate swore he was, maybe that was all the invitation he needed. When he saw the banker leave the door unlocked, maybe he just walked in.

That much Elec might be made to swallow. But how this stranger could have shot the town banker and pulled out of town without a person laying eyes on him — that was the bone that caught in the marshal's throat. He went around behind the bank building and studied the lay of the ground. Now, Nate claimed he saw the man hightailing it out of the side door, probably crossing the street. That being the case, where had the stranger kept his horse?

Blasingame crossed the street where the Ludlow Dry Goods sprawled into the tall weeds of the alley. Not a chance of finding any tracks there; Phil Costain's dray wagon had been back there earlier in the morning.

Anyway, the chance that the killer would run across the street and simply sit tight while the whole town looked for him was a very long one. Not many men had the nerves for that kind of waiting.

There was not an ounce of solid evidence to back up Nate Blaine's story. On the other hand, there was the money that hadn't been found, and Nate's gun, which had been fully loaded when they found him. Those things would be explained easily enough — still, the marshal didn't like the smell of it. He didn't like the doubts that were growing in his mind. Elec headed back to the office to see if Kirk Logan, his day deputy, had showed up yet.

Kirk, a towheaded youngster in his middle twenties, was just strapping on his cartridge belt when the marshal came in. He grinned, but it turned uneasy when he saw the glint in Elec's eyes.

"Sorry I'm late, Elec. But the baby had the croup and I had to rout out Doc Shipley —"

"Never mind," the marshal said shortly. "I want you to round up some men and scour every inch of this town between the bank and the public corral. If that bank money is hidden in Plainsville, I want it. Understand?"

Logan swallowed. "Sure, Elec. I'll get right to work." He turned to go out of the office, but stopped when he reached the steps. "I just thought of something. What if somebody has already found that money?"

Elec's shaggy eyebrows almost covered his eyes as he frowned. The possibility had already occurred to him. He did not try to fool himself — there were plenty of people in Plainsville who would never say anything about it if they found that money. The whole town knew it. The jury would know it. In the light of this knowledge, Nathan Blaine's main line of defense became purely academic.

Blasingame sat solidly at his plank desk for a full minute after his deputy had mounted the steps to the street. Suddenly he hit the desk with his big right fist.

The chances were a thousand to one that Beulah Sewell was telling the truth and that Nate Blaine was guilty as hell. Still, it was that one chance in a thousand that bothered him.

At last he got up and went back to the cell. "Nate," he said, "I'm going to ride over to Landow and get the county sheriff to look for this drifter of yours."

Nathan lay on his bunk, his dark eyes fixed on the ceiling.

"Understand something, Nate," the marshal said. "I think you're guilty as hell. But before I'm through, I'm going to *know* it . . ."

When Blasingame returned from Landow late that night, he learned that his prisoner had escaped. Nathan had flung a cup of scalding coffee in Ralph Striker's face — coffee that the night deputy had paid for and brought to him. During Striker's momentary blindness Nathan had grabbed him through the bars and got his revolver. After forcing the deputy to unlock the cell, Nathan gagged him and locked him in his own cage. Then, at gunpoint, he had taken his horse and rig from the public corral and disappeared in the night.

They formed a posse, of course, but it was a big county and the night was black. They did not find Nathan Blaine.

CHAPTER TEN

A dark cloud of anger rolled over Plainsville when the lawyers came from Landow to make an accounting for Harper's bank. Twelve thousand dollars had been lost in the robbery.

Realization broke upon the town with the suddenness of a winter storm. This loss came out of their own pockets. Townspeople and grim-faced squatters gathered angrily in front of the bank, demanding their money.

The lawyers came out and told them there was nothing they could do. The money was gone. The bank had not been insured. Then they caught the next stage for Landow.

The citizens cast about for an object toward which to hurl their anger, and saw young Jefferson Blaine.

Jeff would not soon forget these next few days and weeks that followed. No promise nor threat nor supplication could bring him out of the house to face those hundreds of angry eyes. The man of pride and swagger had been crushed with one cruel blow, and Jefferson Blaine became a boy again — a frightened boy.

He found no strength in glossy boots of soft black kid, nor in his strong right hand which could aim and fire a Colt's revolver with deadly accuracy.

He did not go the academy that day, nor the two days following. Still, it was not as bad as it might have been. He had never guessed that his Aunt Beulah could be as gentle and understanding as she was then. Not once did she mention his pa, or did she scold him when he locked the door to his bare lean-to cubicle and would not let her in.

That first night — the hardest one — she brought his supper to him. "It's not as bad as you think," she said gently. "Of course people get riled up, but they get over it, too. You don't have to mix with them till you feel like it."

This was the beginning of a new thing.

Until now he had thought of his aunt as a tongue full of sting and spite; his uncle an impatient glare and a pointed order. Now, somehow, they had become people.

Once he had heard his uncle saying, "A bit of understanding — that's fine. But don't spoil the boy, Beulah. This thing he'll have to face out himself."

"Not while I'm alive!" Jeff's aunt had replied.

It was a hard thing to understand, and Jeff did not try to. He accepted their kindness and was grateful.

He did not think about Nathan any more than he had to. At first he was sure that he hated his pa with every fiber of his soul, and he was just as sure that his pa had killed Jed Harper and robbed the bank, and no telling what else. And then he had remembered other things, like the sudden gentleness that sometimes appeared in those dark eyes, and the comforting feel of Nathan's strong, brown hand on Jeff's shoulder. When he thought of these things he became confused and could no longer tell with certainty what was true and what was false.

When at last he did steel himself to leave the house and face the anger of the town, it was not at all the way he had imagined it in his room. Oh, they were angry, all right, but it was something more than that. The boys did not gather in gangs to devil him, as they sometimes did with others who had fallen from favor. When they looked at him, there was more than anger in their eyes.

Their anger was tempered with fear.

It surprised Jeff the first time he saw it. On the third day after Nathan Blaine had disappeared into the prairie night, Jeff faced the world again, wearing a mask of toughness so that the sickness inside him might not show. In the glaring light of day he plodded through the streets of Plainsville, on his way to the academy, as though nothing had happened.

He felt their eyes upon him.

Young Blaine, they were sneering. There goes Nate Blaine's kid.

They could not see the swelling of his throat nor hear the pounding of his heart as he strode before them. It was then that Jeff remembered how his pa had made them cringe, how Nathan had thrown back his head and stared them down with his dark eyes. They had not sneered at his pa. They hadn't dared!

There was something comforting and assuring in this thought. Suddenly Jeff threw back his head in the way he had seen his pa do so many times, and he looked them right in the eye as he passed by on the boardwalk. He walked like a young lion looking for a fight.

The success of his tactics was amazing, even to Jeff. Old Seth Lewellen, whittling in a barrel chair in front of Baxter's store, was the first to break and look in another direction when Jeff passed by. Then Mac Butler, the blacksmith. From some doorway Jeff heard a whispered snarl: "That kid's too damn big for his britches!"

Another voice said, "Maybe you're right. But Nate Blaine's his pa. One thing for sure — I don't want the job of takin' him down. Not while Nate's on the loose!"

Then Jeff began to understand. And he knew that he had nothing to worry about because he was the son of Nathan Blaine!

Oh, they had not forgotten Feyor Jorgenson, who had pulled out of Plainsville in the dark of night. These men who watched him from behind store windows, these clod-busters and store clerks, they would do nothing that might bring the wrath of Nathan Blaine down upon them!

As if by magic, Jeff's sickness disappeared. He filled his lungs with clean, exciting air and suddenly felt like laughing.

Strangely, Jeff no longer had the wish to fight the world, now that he knew it was not necessary. In some mysterious way he could feel Nathan's strong hand on his shoulder, protecting him. He knew that he would never be able to explain it to Wirt, or Beulah, or anyone, and he knew instinctively that it would be better not to try.

His father had gone out of his life as abruptly as he had entered it. The dreamlike days of riding proud beside his pa were over, as were the hours spent in learning the violent ways of guns and the magic of cards.

Jeff was old enough to know that Nathan could never again be a part of his life here in Plainsville. His admiration for that dark-eyed man of violence must be kept locked within himself. The Plainsville people would be a long time forgetting the bank and Jed Harper. A quiet voice in the back of Jeff's mind warned him: they are afraid of Nate Blaine — but don't rub it in.

CHAPTER ELEVEN

Time does not always move in the same direction, but sometimes curves back upon itself and strikes with the fury of a cottonmouth. So time played a perverse prank on Plainsville.

The '70's had come to their violent end. Many of the rowdy trail towns were dying. Texas was being fenced in. The new decade was hailed as an era of peace and prosperity; and the end of outlawry and bloodshed was in sight. Then time, on a frivolous whim, reversed itself; peaceful citizens found themselves on a new frontier as violent as any of the '70's had known.

The railroad came to Plainsville.

Jefferson Blaine, now eighteen, watched in amazement as the settlement reverted to the loud and brassy times that he had so longed for as a boy. First came the surveyors, and there was great excitement in the town. The railroad was an unmistakable sign of progress, the store-keepers happily proclaimed.

The railroad meant new markets for the grangers — and there was a flurry of business at the new Farmers Bank as the homesteaders hurried to replace worn-out tools and equipment. New business houses were established. There arose a new eating house —

competition to the Paradise — a new barn at the public corral, and another saloon. Sam Baxter and Frank Ludlow talked of putting up a hotel.

Then came the graders, building a raw mound of earth across the prairie; a track bed, they called it. Then came the track layers themselves, the broad-shouldered spike maulers, the Irish gandy dancers. The new depot was not even finished when the twin glistening rails were hammered to the earth directly in front of Mike Bender's feed store.

Before the town had finished celebrating, carpenters had already gone to work building chutes and cattle pens to the south of town.

Now, once again, there was loud laughter in Plainsville, and the cowhands raced their horses in the streets. Gunfire was no longer a rare sound, and tinny piano music clamored in the saloons. Strange women appeared from nowhere and mixed with the cowhands wherever they drank or gambled. Swift and Blackwelder, a pair of undertakers from Dodge, rented space from Doc Shipley and waited for business.

The transformation was shocking to some, pleasing to others. Plainsville had become a shipping center for cattle, and the ranchers soon forgot their oath to stay away.

For Jeff Blaine, the eternal noise of the place was a delight. It was like stepping from the grave into the middle of a Mexican fiesta. From the workbench in his uncle's tin shop he could see the boiling seas of cattle that descended upon Plainsville like flash floods in April. Their bawling and horn clacking and stamping added to the general din and atmosphere of excitement. Cowhands from the big outfits, heavy with guns, fresh from the new bath house and barber shop, prowled the streets like happy tigers.

This was an August day; the air was furnace-dry and heavy with dust. Jeff lay aside his heavy cutting shears and stood looking out with vague discontent. Since finishing his schooling at the academy he had worked here in Wirt's tin shop. Five years, almost. You'd think a man would get used to his work in that length of time.

Sometimes he thought of his father with sadness. Nathan's name was never mentioned in the Sewell household, but stories had a way of traveling in this country, and Jeff had heard some of the them.

They said his pa was someplace in Mexico, a personal bodyguard for a high man in the Mexican army. They said that Nate Blaine was a big man in Mexico, which was why Texas authorities couldn't try him for killing Jed Harper.

They said a lot of things about Nate Blaine — but not to Jeff's face. Eighteen was a man's age in this country. The name of Blaine kept most of them at a distance.

Jeff watched Elec Blasingame, a bit fatter, a bit thicker, cross the dusty street and head toward the tin shop. It seemed to Jeff that the marshal had grown old fast, since the railroad came to town. That bulldog jaw had gone flabby. It look longer to kindle the fierce fire in those pale eyes.

Now the marshal stood in the tinshop doorway. "Is your uncle here, Jeff?"

"I think he went over to Baxter's. Anything I can help you with, Marshal?"

"No." He wiped his face with his sleeve. Both of them remembered too much, and neither was comfortable. "If I don't run on him in the street, tell Wirt to come down to my office, will you?"

"All right." Jeff put a note of curiosity in the words, but Elec chose to ignore it. He glanced at Jeff for one brief moment — a strange, almost bewildered look.

Elec said abruptly, "You like it here in the tinshop, Jeff?"

"Sure. It's all right, I guess."

The marshal's fat jowls shook as he nodded. "Good business Wirt's got here. It'll be yours some day, I figure."

Jeff wondered what he was getting at. In five years he couldn't remember passing more than a dozen words with Blasingame. Why the sudden interest? "I hadn't thought much about it," he said. "But I guess I'm the only one Uncle Wirt's got to leave anything to — except Aunt Beulah, of course."

"Of course," Elec said, cocking his head slightly, as though he were listening for something. Then he looked directly at Jeff, with some of the old fire in his eyes. "They've been good to you," he said bluntly. "Wirt and Beulah. I hope you don't forget it."

Now that was a funny thing for him to say, Jeff thought, as Elec shoved away from the door and tramped heavily up the street.

A few minutes later Wirt came in and Jeff told him about the marshal's visit. "I wonder what Elec wants to see me about?" Wirt pondered. "Well, I guess I'll have to go to his office."

If Wirt Sewell could have seen the look of stark savageness in the marshal's eyes at that moment, he would not have been so pleased with himself as he marched primly toward the Masonic Temple building.

But the marshal was a block away, in his office, alone, when he read the letter through for the fourth time. In a fit of helpless rage, he balled the letter in one big fist and hurled it at the wall.

He stood spread-legged, mean as a bear, in the center of his bleak office. He looked as though he would happily kill the first man who dared come down the steps.

But by the time Wirt Sewell reached the Masonic Temple building, Elec had control of himself. He sat heavy and expressionless at his plank desk.

Five years hadn't done much to change Wirt Sewell. He was the same tight-wound little man that he had been since his late twenties. Today he was at peace with the world. Business was good at the tin shop and the town was booming. Of course there was the bawdy element of the town that was a curse to all respectable citizens, but Wirt allowed the town would tame down before long. He had seen it happen before. When all the ruffians were gone, or killed, Plainsville would still be standing, a thriving city.

A faint smile played at the corners of Wirt's mouth as he crossed the street. He'd had quite a surprise today; Sam Baxter and Frank Ludlow had asked him to throw in with them on the new hotel they were planning. And

Baxter and Ludlow were just about the most important businessmen in Plainsville.

At first Wirt had been puzzled as to why they had come to him for help. "Why, Wirt," Frank Ludlow had said, "you're one of the most successful men in this town, that's why we came to you. You started with a little hole-in-the-wall place here and made it into a big payin' tin shop. I guess you just don't realize how successful you really are!"

Wirt could still hear those words, and the flow of well-being warmed him. Maybe Frank hadn't been so wrong, at that, he thought. He and Beulah had put some money aside. They had raised Jeff as well as they knew how, seeing the boy through that hard year after his pa had stirred up so much trouble. No sir, the Sewell's didn't have much to be ashamed of. And the boy was a big help at the shop — a good, steady worker, once he'd set his mind to it.

Wirt hadn't decided yet about the hotel. He'd have to talk it over with Beulah. But the fact that Frank and Sam had asked him put a new spring in his step, made him feel years younger.

For the first time in Wirt Sewell's plodding, unexciting life, he timidly began laying the shimmering foundation for a dream.

Now he made his way down the stone steps to the Masonic Temple basement. He walked into Elec Blasingame's office, only faintly curious as to why the marshal wanted to see him. He said pleasantly, "Hello, Elec. Jeff said you wanted to talk to me about something."

The marshal said bluntly, "Sit down, Wirt."

There was something about his tone that made Wirt blink; there was something in the steely cast of Elec's eyes that hinted trouble. Wirt realized that the marshal had not asked him here for just a friendly gab fest.

Without hesitation, Wirt cut himself away from the pleasantness of his dream. He pulled up a chair and sat down.

Blasingame leaned heavily on his elbows, his thick mouth drawn sharply down at the corners. "I'll come right out with it, Wirt. I've got some news you won't like to hear. I've got a letter here from the county sheriff in Landow — it didn't come from the sheriff, but from a deputy marshal up in the Choctaw Nation . . ."

Wirt frowned. He thought he knew what Elec was trying to say. "It's about Nate, isn't it?"

"Nate Blaine?" Something curious happened behind the marshal's eyes. "Yes, it has something to do with Nate, but not in the way you think, maybe. This deputy worked out of Fort Smith, but he was on the trail of a killer that had disappeared in the Nations. He found his man, finally, hiding out with the Choctaws, and had to kill him."

Wirt broke in. "Does this have anything to do with me?"

"This is what it has to do with you, Wirt." Elec's voice went harsh. "Before this hardcase died, he confessed to killing Jed Harper in that bank robbery five years back."

The implication left Wirt numb.

"He still had some of the money with him," Blasingame went on coldly. "A lone rider doesn't have much chance to spend twelve thousand dollars, I guess. Anyway, he had it, in those canvas bags that banks use."

The chill of dread showed on Wirt's face.

"It's a lie!" he said tightly. "Nate Blaine killed Harper and took the money!"

Elec's voice cut like a winter wind. "It's no lie. A death-bed confession is the strongest evidence there is, and you know it, Wirt. Besides, those canvas bags I mentioned — they were stenciled with the name of Harper's bank."

Wirt Sewell had ceased to be one of Plainsville's most successful businessmen; the flow of well-being no longer warmed him. He was now an old, bewildered man, his senses skating on the thin edge of panic.

"But Beulah saw him! It had to be Nate!"

"It wasn't Nate." The marshal's voice was almost a snarl. "And your wife didn't see him. It was all cooked up inside her head. Out of spite, out of meanness . . . God only knows why a woman would do a thing like that!"

In sudden anger, Blasingame shoved himself away from the desk and paced wildly up and down the office floor. "Five years!" he said bitterly. "That's how long it's been. Five years of hiding, of being afraid to come back to his own country, even to see his boy. How Nathan must hate us, Wirt — all of us, for I was in it, too. I was the one who took Beulah's word for it and locked him up."

Wirt's face was gray. His mouth moved, but no sound was made. The marshal turned on him and said harshly, "Well, that's what I wanted to tell you, Wirt. That's all there is to it."

The marshal took his anger in a heavy hand. He breathed deeply, giving himself time to settle down. At last he said, "I shouldn't fly off the handle like that, it's bad for my blood pressure. Just forget what I said, Wirt."

"Forget?" Wirt looked at him. "What am I going to do, Elec? How can Beulah stand up to a thing like this?"

"I don't figure that's the question. How is the boy going to stand up to it?"

It was well past sundown when Jeff came home to the Sewell house that night. He came in the front door as usual and hung his hat on the tree in the hall. At first he didn't notice the unusual silence.

"I locked the shop," he called toward the kitchen. "When Uncle Wirt didn't come back —"

That was when he noticed the unnatural quiet of the room — it seemed to be an uneasy hush. Jeff frowned, listening for the familiar sounds that were not there, the rattle of pans, the shaking of the grate in the cookstove. But there was only silence — and still he could feel that the house was not empty.

He walked across the small parlor and into the kitchen, and there was Wirt sitting at the table, seeming even more shrunken and smaller than usual, his face grayer. Beulah was standing beside the cookstove staring dully straight ahead.

Jeff's frown deepened. He shot a quick glance at Beulah, then at Wirt. "What's the matter?"

Wirt cleared his throat, but did not look toward the door where Jeff was standing. "Jeff, you'd better sit down."

Then the hush came down again, but it was not a passive silence. The very air seemed to crackle. The muteness that had seized his aunt and uncle began to rub on Jeff's nerves. "What's the matter here?" he said again, looking at Wirt. "You didn't come back to the shop. Now I come home and find you and Aunt Beulah looking like you were holding a wake." When they made no sound, his impatience grew more demanding. "I want to know what's wrong!"

Then, for the first time, Wirt looked up at him. "Jeff, there's something we've got to tell you . . ."

"No!" The sound was small and thin, almost a wail. Jeff turned quickly to see his aunt cover her face with her hands.

Wirt sighed heavily. "It's no use, Beulah. He'll hear it anyway. Better for it to come from us."

Jeff was aware of an excited hammering in his chest, and then a sudden silence, as though his heart had stopped its beating. "Is it something about Pa? Is that the trouble?"

Wirt glanced quickly at his wife. "Yes —" he said — "It's something about your pa, Jeff."

"Then what is it?"

Wirt sat perfectly still, his eyes faded and old. "Do you remember the business about the bank, Jeff? When Jed Harper was killed?"

The hammering began again in Jeff's chest. "I remember."

"And how your Aunt Beulah identified Nate as the killer?"

For five long years he had trained himself not to think of that day. He had smothered the fire of his anger in the darkest part of his mind, and he had thought until now that the fire was dead. Now he drew himself tall and straight. He said coldly, as though he already knew: "Go on."

Wirt saw that he could stall no longer. "It appears," he said quietly, "that Beulah made a mistake that day."

The working of the mind is a strange thing. Sometimes it accepts only the things it wants to accept and rejects all others — and that is the way it was with Jeff at that moment. He heard the words but could not make himself accept their meaning.

He said stiffly, "I don't know what you're talking about."

But everything about him, from the rigidity of his body to the iron-hard cast of his face, said that he knew. And Wirt saw that telling him was going to be more difficult than he had imagined.

"It was a mistake, Jeff," Wirt said. "I know it was a terrible thing for Nate, but mistakes sometimes happen. Your aunt simply mistook another man for your pa."

It was strange that he felt no anger; there was only shock and emptiness as full realization forced its way through the barriers of his mind. It was the wounded man's instant of numbness before the pain begins. He turned slowly away from Wirt and faced his aunt.

"Was it a mistake, Aunt Beulah?"

Beulah could not take her hands from in front of her face. She could not look at him.

"Was it a mistake, Aunt Beulah, or did you do it on purpose?"

She ducked her head quickly, like a child that had been scolded. To Jeff the gesture seemed ridiculous. Then her shoulders began to jerk and he knew that he was seeing his aunt cry for the first time in his life, and that seemed ridiculous too. Suddenly Beulah made that thin little wailing sound again. She threw her apron over her face and ran blindly from the room.

There was a look of worry, almost fear, in Wirt's eyes as he quickly shoved himself up from the table. "Jeff, whatever she did, she did because she loved you. She didn't want anything to hurt you."

Jeff turned and looked at Wirt without actually seeing him. Then he turned and walked stiffly out of the kitchen and through the parlor. The front door closed quietly, and Wirt Sewell bent over the table and struck it several times with his fist . . .

A shocking thing happened later that night.

The regular Saturday-night dance on the second floor of the Masonic Temple building was going full swing when Jeff Blaine arrived half drunk and mean, spoiling for a fight. When one of the Cross 4 hands asked Amy Wintworth to dance, Jeff hit him full in the face with his fist. A brawl was started and Elec

Blasingame and his night deputy had to break it up, barring all Cross 4 men from the hall and locking Jeff up until he cooled off.

"Blood will tell!" the dancers sniffed in disgust.

"Young Blaine — exactly like his pa! They'll both hang at the end of a rope before it's over!"

Elec and Ralph Striker wrestled Jeff out of the hall fighting and kicking, swearing to kill every man in sight. When Amy Wintworth tried to talk to him, he snarled like a tiger.

Striker had his big right fist cocked. "Let me take care of this young tough, Elec!"

"Let him alone!" the marshal snapped. Together, they fought him down the stairway, down to the basement and into the cell.

"What that kid needs," Striker said angrily, "is a good beating."

"Ralph," the marshal answered wearily, feeling the heavy weight of his age, "I figure young Blaine has taken enough beating for one day. Go back to the dance and keep the boys under control. And," he added, "see if you can find Amy Wintworth — that's Ford Wintworth's girl. Tell her I want to see her."

A few minutes later Amy and her brother Todd came timidly into the marshal's office. Elec brightened a bit, for he was not so old that he could not appreciate the freshness and beauty of young womanhood. "Thanks for coming, Amy. And you too, Todd. If young Blaine has any friends in Plainsville, I guess it's you two. And he needs friends now about as much as anybody I ever saw."

Todd shook his head with a solemn, bitter smile. "Sometimes I wonder if it's possible to be Jeff's friend." He laughed quietly, without humor. "It's like trying to tame a coyote. No matter how well you think you know him, he's sure to snap at you when you least expect it."

"And you, Amy?" Elec said quietly. "Long as I can remember, almost, you've been seein' quite a lot of Jeff Blaine. Do you think he's a wild thing that can't be tamed?"

Amy's eyes were wide and hurt by what had happened. A tall, graceful girl with gentle features, she dropped her gaze and murmured, "No, I don't think that."

"You like him, don't you?" Elec asked bluntly. And when color suddenly came to her cheeks, he said with surprising gentleness, "Never mind an old man's clumsy questions. Sit down, both of you."

Amy and her brother sat uneasily on the edges of leather-bottom chairs, and Elec Blasingame wondered where all the years had gone. It seemed only yesterday that they had been children — now Todd was a young man, and his sister was old enough to think about getting a husband. Now, with these two youngsters before him, Elec felt vaguely restless and did not know what to say. He wasted a minute lighting a frayed cigar, and then turned to Amy.

"Maybe I'm just an old fool," he said. "In a way, I'm responsible for the way Jeff Blaine acted tonight. I won't tell you why — more than likely, though, the story will be around town by tomorrow. Anyway, I've got no right to ask you and your brother to help patch up a mistake of mine. If you want to leave, it's all right."

Amy and Todd looked puzzled, and did not move.

Amy asked quietly, "Is there something I should know, Marshal?"

"Yes, Amy, but it's not my right to tell you. All I can do is ask you to try to understand young Blaine. He's had a hard knock — he'll need all the help he can get."

Todd, with a touch of self-righteousness in his voice, said, "There's no excuse for what Jeff did tonight. The Mason's dance is the only place left for decent people in Plainsville, and he did his best to ruin that. If he's going to behave like a dancehall tough, then let him hang out in Bert Surratt's place."

The marshall sighed. "I was afraid that's the way you'd take it."

"And I don't think it would be good for Amy to see so much of Jeff," Todd added with a note of male authority.

Elec noticed that Amy's back stiffened, although she did not look in Todd's direction. She came to her feet, smiling faintly. "Todd, perhaps you should take me home." She added to the marshal: "Thank you for what you tried to do for Jeff. I understand more than you might think."

Blasingame sat in deep thought after Amy Wintworth and her brother disappeared up the steps to the street. He was disappointed with his efforts to get the Blaine boy straightened out. He could only hope that Amy Wintworth was wiser and more understanding than he had any right to believe a young girl could be.

CHAPTER TWELVE

In the middle of the block, on a dusty, nameless cross street, the Wintworth house stood proud and glistening in its new dress of white paint. Ford Wintworth, a lean, sharp-faced man, stood on his front porch smoking an after-dinner pipe. A dazzling sun beat down on the red clay and frame houses — hot, even for August — and Ford wondered vaguely if there would be a dry-up in the hills.

It was time to be getting back to the wagon yard where he worked, but he kept finding excuses to put off the moment of departure. There was worry in Ford's quick brown eyes as he stared out at the haze of dust that hung over Main Street; there was uneasiness in his stance.

The story had made all the rounds by now, about how they had wrongly accused Nate Blaine of murder and robbery. Ford Wintworth had heard it a dozen times — every man had his own version of what had happened. Ford had noted with some interest how, at first, the people had felt the hand of shame upon them, especially the ones who had been so strong for lynching. Then, in some ingenious way, they had converted their shame to anger, which they aimed at Beulah Sewell.

In a completely impersonal way, Ford felt sorry for Beulah, for he knew that she would pay many times over for what she had done. The citizens of Plainsville did not like being shown off as fools, and they would not soon forget.

The Sewells, however, held only a minor place in Ford Wintworth's interests. It was his daughter who worried him. Oh, he had known for a long time that Amy had been casting glances in Jeff Blaine's direction, but he had figured it was a schoolgirl thing and amounted to nothing. Until a day or so ago Ford had thought of his daughter as still a little girl, and it shocked him slightly to realize that she was a young woman with a mind of her own — and old enough to think of marriage.

Todd, who now worked for his father at the corral, came out to the porch. "I'll walk with you as far as the bank, Pa."

"I'm not going to the yard just yet," Ford said. "Todd, tell me something, will you?" Then he rubbed the stubble on his face, not knowing exactly how to say it. "What I mean is —"

His son smiled faintly. "I think I know. It's Amy and Jeff Blaine."

Ford was surprised that his son could read him so clearly. "I didn't know it showed. But you're right. Look here, Todd, is Amy serious about this Blaine boy?"

His son shrugged. "It looks that way. After that affair at the dance, I thought maybe she'd be cured. But I guess I don't know much about women."

Todd took makings from his shirt pocket and thoughtfully rolled a thin cigarette in his lean, brown fingers. He looked as though he wanted to say something more, then thought better of it and merely nodded. "I guess I'd better get on to the corral, Pa. You going to talk to Amy about this?"

Ford grunted, and didn't answer.

Several minutes later Ford was still on the porch when his daughter came outside. "Pa, I thought you'd gone back to work."

Ford hesitated, feeling ridiculous. The subtle approach was not a part of the Wintworth make-up, and finally he blurted: "Damn it, Amy, I want to talk to you about this Blaine boy."

A shade of caution seemed to lower behind his daughter's eyes. But she only said, "All right, Pa."

"I'll come right out with it," Ford stated. "I don't think you ought to be seeing young Blaine any more. His reputation was none too good to start with, and it's getting worse every day. That business at the dance was bad enough, but now he's taken to carrying a gun and hanging out in Bert Surratt's place. Amy, I don't believe you ought to see him any more."

His daughter said quietly, "You aren't ordering me not to see Jeff, are you, Pa?"

Ford Wintworth was far from deaf. He heard the warning tone in Amy's voice with perfect clarity and it brought him up short. He looked at his daughter as though he had never seen her before.

"You know I wouldn't order you to do anything," Ford said nervously.

Amy smiled. Suddenly she kissed her father on the cheek. "Don't worry so much about me, Pa. I'm not a young girl who doesn't know what she's doing. I'm a woman."

For the first time in his life, Ford Wintworth had lost the upper hand with one of his children, but he was smart enough to know it. He murmured something and tried to give the impression that everything was fine and that nothing had changed. As he started back toward town he walked a bit straighter than usual, with great dignity. But within his own mind he knew that his daughter had defeated him.

On the porch of the Wintworth house, Amy also knew that she had won, for the moment. But the victory was not sweet. It is only the beginning, she thought soberly. More lines will be drawn, more battles fought.

Amy loved her father, and her brother, and she had no wish to hurt them or fight with them. But she was also a woman and she knew what she wanted.

Amy still shrank within herself whenever she remembered Jeff Blaine's actions of a week ago. She had been so angry at the time that she swore to herself that she would never speak to him again . . . but that was before Elec Blasingame had talked to her — before she had heard the story of Beulah Sewell and what she had done to Jeff's father and to Jeff.

Now she could understand the rage that Jeff Blaine had unleashed that night. She could not condone it, but she could live with it for a little while, until the rage had burned itself out.

Mrs. Wintworth, a onetime beauty who had grown heavy and placid, came to the front door. "Amy, there are dinner dishes to be done."

"All right, Mother."

"Didn't I hear your father out here?"

"Yes, but he's gone now." Amy was sure that her mother had heard everything that had been said. But Mrs. Wintworth chose to believe that no problem existed and that Jefferson Blaine was merely a name that came up now and then in quilting gossip. In a vague sort of way Mrs. Wintworth foresaw her daughter marrying one of the acceptable, well-to-do boys of Plainsville and living out her days in a white frame house exactly like the one Ford Wintworth had built for himself and his family — and Amy had learned long ago that it was just as well to let her mother believe what she would.

"All right, Mother," Amy said again and turned to go in the house.

"Isn't that buggy stopping at our gate, Amy?" Mrs. Wintworth asked.

Amy turned, surprised to see Jeff Blaine draw up at the front gate in a glistening black buggy. Hurriedly, Mrs. Wintworth ducked back into the house, but Amy knew that she would be listening on the other side of the door. Jeff sat for a moment, a tight little smile playing at the corners of his mouth.

"Am I welcome?" he asked.

It was the first Amy had seen of him since the night of the dance. "Of course," she said quietly, betraying none of the excitement that hammered within her.

It had always been so. Jeff Blaine could look at her and her blood would race through her veins. Even as children, when he had elaborately refused to admit that she was alive, it had been so. Amy Wintworth understood it better now than she had then.

Abruptly, with nervous quickness, Jeff vaulted out of the buggy and walked unsmiling to the gate. Amy felt something cry out within herself when she saw the tense, hard lines around his mouth. He was so young — and looked so old! Since the coming of the railroad, armed men were no longer novelties in Plainsville, but the sight of the heavy revolver on Jeff's right thigh frightened her. She hoped the fear did not show in her face when she swung open the gate and asked quietly, "Won't you come in?"

"I'm not sure your folks would like it," he said stiffly.

"You didn't come to see my folks, did you?"

He did not smile. He looked as though he had forgotten how. "I guess," he said grimly, "I ought to apologize for — for what happened at the dance."

His voice and his face are so hard, Amy thought. But she said in the same quiet voice, "Not unless you want to."

"Well, I apologize." As though he were reading it from a book. "I didn't mean for you to get mixed up in it." They stood for a moment in uneasy silence. Then he added, "I rented this rig for the rest of the day. I thought maybe you'd like to ride over toward Stone Ridge with me."

Amy's eyes widened in surprise. "Stone Ridge?"

"I won a piece of land over there last night. I thought I might as well see what it looks like."

So he has won some land, Amy thought slowly. Over a gambling table in Bert Surratt's place, probably. A little chill went over her, and she saw for the first time how much he resembled his father.

"Of course," he said bluntly, "if you don't want to go . . ."

But Amy knew that she would go. Never in her life had she turned down one of Jeff Blaine's rare invitations. She said, "I'll have to get a bonnet, and tell Mother."

Mrs. Wintworth looked at her daughter in dismay. "Stone Ridge! Amy, the whole town will talk!"

"The town will talk anyway," Amy said. Then she turned to her mother and added gently, "Don't you see? He's hurt and angry and thinks the whole world is his enemy. If I turned against him now, there's no telling what he'd do."

Her mother blinked in disbelief. "Amy, you can't mean that you actually care what happens to a ruffian like Jeff Blaine!"

Amy's face turned blank as she put on her bonnet. "I'll do the dishes when I get back," she said quietly.

They rode in silence along Main Street. Heads turned to watch as they passed. Amy could feel their disapproving stares. She could almost hear their clucking tongues as they shook their heads from side to side. The corners of Jeff's mouth lifted slightly in a cold, humorless smile.

They took the old stage road out of town and headed north toward the hills. The parched land lay spread out before them, dazzling yellow and shimmering in the sun. There was a great silence broken only by buggy wheels and hoofs, and now and then a field lark's cry. Some of that big country's lonesomeness fell around Amy as the noisy activity of the town fell behind them.

Amy found herself thinking back to other times, to the years of her childhood. She found herself watching Jeff Blaine's hard young face, wondering what it was about those intense eyes and thin mouth that had always drawn her to him.

Being wise in so many things, it was strange that she understood so little of the man himself. Amy, whose young will could control a headstrong man like Ford Wintworth, learned early that the harder you held to Jeff Blaine the easier he slipped away. He was quicksilver; he was mystery. And within his strong body was locked the secret of his own doom.

Much of this was foolishness, of course, the product of a romantic girl's too-active imagination, and in an objective way Amy knew it. Certainly there was nothing mysterious about a barefoot boy who was too muleheaded and stubborn to come to one of her parties — the kind of boy Jeff had once been, before Nathan Blaine had filled him with his own importance, spoiled him and brought to life an arrogance and violence that most men were content to leave sleeping.

In her quiet way, Amy hated Nathan Blaine. She hated the man's arrogance, and the way he had tossed his big head and stared down at you with those dark eyes. Most of all she hated him for the bragging bully that he had made of his own son, and for this she would not forgive him.

In Amy's cold, woman's logic, she could almost admire Beulah Sewell for the thing she had done. With Nathan out of his life, Jeff had become a boy again with normal feelings and emotions.

Now Amy wished for the impossible. Gladly would she have stood up for Beulah's lie, but she knew that it would only bring Jeff's rage down upon her. And besides, lies were not practical. Despite all good intent, their cut was cruel when they were found out, as Beulah Sewell came to know.

Still, Amy admired Beulah's courage. Beulah had seen what Nathan Blaine was doing to the boy and she had done what she could to stop it.

At the moment it did not occur to Amy that Beulah had self-righteously taken the law into her own hands. The end, it seemed to Amy, was worth the means, and that the plan had failed was its only fault.

Now, as the buggy rolled across that wide prairie, Amy gazed out over the shaggy grassland dotted here and there with patches of nester corn. Jeff had not said more than a dozen words since the town had fallen behind them, but now he waved abruptly toward the fields of corn.

"Good grassland. Soon it'll all be plowed up and blown away."

That was what the cattlemen had been saying since the first nester sank his dugout in Landow County, but the land was still there and the corn thrived. Amy looked at him, but said nothing. Sooner or later he would get around to telling her of other things. She was good at waiting.

"There's Stone Ridge," he said after a while, pointing to a hogback hump of scrub and sandstone in the distance. "Two sections over there somewhere were deeded to me this morning. Not much to graze beef cattle on, but it's something."

Amy spoke for the first time. "Two sections is a lot of land to some people. You haven't said how you got it."

Jeff shot her a quick glance. "I told you I won it. At poker, from a nester."

Amy felt that small chill go over her again, and she looked away from those intense eyes that reminded her so much of his father. She heard herself saying quietly, "I didn't know you were such a good gambler."

"Good?" He laughed shortly. "I was lucky. I'm no great shakes as a gambler right now, but I'll learn. My pa said I had a natural talent for it."

"Oh," she said softly, but if he heard the note of dismay in her voice, he did not show it. "Is that what you mean to make of yourself, a gambler?"

Now he did look at her, levelly. "Is there anything wrong with that?"

Her voice sounded weak. "I don't know. I've never known any gamblers."

"Maybe you'd like me to do something else," he said shortly. "Maybe I could learn to clean your pa's stables."

The tone of his voice angered her. "You don't have to clean stables," she replied cuttingly. "Your uncle was good enough to teach you a trade."

He grew rigid, high color flushing his cheeks. "I don't want to talk about the Sewells! I don't want to hear their name mentioned!"

They rode in stiff, uncomfortable silence for several minutes. At last he said, "Amy, I didn't mean to bark at you. I'm sorry."

But it was not the same after that. Amy was angry with herself for coming with him; doubly angry because she knew that she would do it all over again if he asked her. She tilted her chin haughtily and refused to speak to him or look in his direction.

"Well, there it is," Jeff said flatly when they reached the ridge. There was a broad valley on the western side of the scrubby slope. The land was a thick carpet of grass, dotted here and there with cottonwoods and willows that grew along a shallow creek. Jeff was surprised at the lushness of his new holdings. Amy saw a boyish excitement in his face as he dismounted from the buggy and stood looking down at the spread of grass. Despite her determination to stay angry, she felt herself thawing.

"Look at that!" he said huskily. "Grass belly-high on a four-year-old steer, and that nester was trying to farm it!"

He handed Amy down from the buggy and both of them stood on the edge of the ridge gazing down in amazement. Amy pointed toward the opposite slope. "Isn't that a house over there?"

"The nester's shack, I guess. Already falling down."

"It doesn't look as if it had been farmed," Amy said, puzzled.

"That's why the nester was willing to gamble it. Too lazy to make enough improvements to hold it."

"And now it's yours?" she asked, as though she was trying to get used to the idea.

It was then that they saw the lone horseman streaking across the flatland to the west. Both of them watched the trail of dust kick up over the prairie and slowly drift away with the wind. The rider's strong gray covered ground fast and soon disappeared in the afternoon sun behind the ridge.

Jeff glanced at Amy and shrugged. "A poor way to treat horseflesh in this kind of heat. Well, I guess we've seen all there is to see." They returned to the buggy, turned around on the rocky slope and headed slowly back to Plainsville.

Out of curiosity, Amy looked back over her shoulder as they neared the stage road, but there was no sign of the lone rider. She dismissed the incident from her mind and turned her imagination to that valley of grass that now belonged to Jeff. She could close her eyes and almost see a neat, white painted house there on the green slope, and cattle rolling in fat grazing contentedly in the deep grass along the creek. She visualized the beginning of a new brand in Texas — the Blaine brand.

"Jeff, what are you going to do with that land?"

He snapped the lines over the horse's back and clucked his tongue. "I don't know yet. Sell it, maybe. Two sections of land's not good for anything but farming, and I'm not a sodbuster."

"I didn't expect anything," she said, but Jeff could see that she had. They rode for a while in silence, and when Jeff tried to take her hand, she pulled away from him. Angrily, Jeff kept his eyes on the road ahead. He wished that he could forget Amy Wintworth. He could never please her. She always wanted the impossible.

But he no longer denied that he liked being with her. She was not easy to get along with, but she was always there when he needed her, which was more than he could say for anybody else. Even his pa.

Oh, she got mad at him sometimes, but she didn't stay mad. Like that affair with the Jorgensons, and the fight at the dance. She could cut like a whip when riled, but he didn't mind that so much because she always got over it.

Only recently had Jeff begun to realize that things between himself and Amy were not the same as they had always been. Not for several years had he thought up elaborate schemes to ignore her; now he found himself thinking up excuses to be with her. For a long while a thought had been growing in his mind. Despite the fact that they often fought and she was almost impossible to please, the feeling that he would never be able to forget her had grown stronger and stronger within him. At last he had admitted it to himself, grudgingly — he guessed that he was in love with Amy Wintworth.

It was not an easy thought to live with. For one thing, Ford Wintworth was against it — and Todd, too, who used to be Jeff's friend.

Sometimes when Jeff thought about it an emptiness grew inside him until he felt that he was nothing but a hollow shell, lost and desperate. Too much of his life had been spent in anger, there had been too many reasons for hate. Today he could walk the streets of Plainsville, up and down and across, and never meet a person he could call a friend.

They feared him because of his pa and because his name was Blaine, despised him for his shield of arrogance; some hated him for what they themselves had done to Nathan. Grizzled cattlemen would make room for him at a gambling table because of his gun and reputation; Bert Surratt would serve him at the bar for the same reason. But not one of them was his friend. Only Amy understood him.

At times he wanted to tell her the things he felt. He wanted to show her what right he had to hate this town and everybody in it; but if spoken, the words would never sound the way he heard them in his mind, so he kept his thoughts to himself.

Some day he would think of a way to settle with Beulah and Wirt Sewell. He would think of a plan to even the score with all the others who sneered at him. Some day his anger would spill over and he would be rid of it, and then perhaps he could tell Amy all the things he wanted her to know.

As the buggy jolted along the deep rutted stage road, Jeff was surprised to see a group of horsemen break out of a stand of brush and head toward them.

Amy looked at him. "Isn't that Elec Blasingame in front?"

"Looks like it," Jeff said flatly.

"Aren't you going to stop? They're headed in this direction."

Something in Jeff's face went hard. "If they want to talk to us, they can catch up. I don't figure I'm in debt to any law in Plainsville."

Amy did not show surprise. In a way she could understand Jeff's hostile attitude, because of what had happened to his father. Looking back she saw the horsemen spur to a gallop as they moved west toward the stage road to cut them off. There were seven of them, all Plainsville citizens, headed by Marshal Blasingame and his day deputy, Kirk Logan.

"Thanks for waiting for us," Logan said with dry anger as the group reined up alongside the buggy.

"You're welcome," Jeff said flatly, and color rose in the deputy's face.

Then Blasingame kneed his mount in on the inside, between Jeff and Logan. "None of that!" he said shortly, after touching his hatbrim to Amy. "We're looking for a man, Blaine. Heavy-set, about forty. We followed his trail this way out of town but lost it on the shale bed to the south of here. You happen to see anybody to fit the description?"

Jeff raked the riders with a glance, noting the ropes and rifles. "Was he riding a gray?" he asked mildly.

"By hell, that's the one!" Kirk Logan said. "Where'd you see him?"

"Can't say what the rider looked like; he was too far off. Me and Amy were over toward Stone Ridge. Saw him scooting across the prairie like he had a burr under his tail."

Blasingame wiped his sweaty face on his sleeve. "Sounds like the one, all right. Which direction was he headed?"

"East," Jeff said casually. "Due east."

As he said it, he shot a glance at Amy, stopping the words that were on her lips.

"Thanks, Blaine," the marshal said, and the riders began pulling their horses around. "He won't get away from us now."

"Wait!" Amy called. But she was too late. The marshal and his posse were pounding back to the east and her voice was lost in the thunder of hoofs. She fixed Jeff with her flashing eyes. "The man we saw was headed west! You know he was!"

She hardly recognized the man beside her as the Jeff Blaine she had ridden with from Plainsville. "There are a lot of gray horses in Texas," he said coldly. "Maybe he was the wrong man."

"But what if he was the right man? What if he's a killer?"

Jeff took her arm and tried to make his voice gentle. "Amy, I'm not the law; that's Elec's job. But remember that I saw them catch the wrong man once and try to hang him. I'm not going to help them catch another one."

Amy felt futility well up inside her, knowing that nothing she could say would erase his bitterness. An uneasy wall built up between them as the buggy rolled again toward Plainsville. "Jeff," she said at last, "my father talked to me today. He asked me not to see you again."

Jeff shot her a glance, waiting for her to go on.

"Maybe he was right," she said, and he held his silence.

CHAPTER THIRTEEN

The name the stranger gave was Bill Somerson; he had arrived in Plainsville on the noon mail train the day before. Very little was know about him except that he had come well heeled, and was looking for action at Bert Surratt's poker tables. With the wisdom of hindsight, Surratt confessed later that Somerson had a mean look to him and he wasn't surprised when Phil Costain caught him with a holdout up his sleeve. After the holdout discovery, the stranger shot Costain in the groin, stole thc gray from the hitch rack outside the saloon and fogged it out of town. The most surprising thing, the saloonkeeper claimed, was that Costain was still alive to tell it.

Jeff heard the story when he returned from Stone Ridge shortly before sundown. The loafers around the livery barn were full of it when he turned in his hired rig.

To Jeff, it was just another shooting. They were not rare in Plainsville these days. He was still mad at himself for not patching up the fight with Amy before letting her out at her house. But like mules, both of them had refused to give, and they had parted in anger.

If she can't understand the reasons I have for hating this town, he told himself, maybe it's just as well I find it out now.

But he didn't believe it. As he walked toward town from the livery barn, he felt his anger leaving him, the ache of loneliness pulling at his nerves. He tramped the plank walk to the Paradise eating house and made his supper on stew and sourdough bread. He had the thought to go back to the Wintworth house and make it up with her, but he didn't know what to say. Anyway, Ford would probably want to put in his own word and make him madder than he already was.

Well, he told himself, she'll get over it.

But this time he wondered. He had not liked the look of hurt in her eyes, the coldness with which she had drawn away from him. He dropped some silver on the counter and walked out of the restaurant.

The sun had died behind the lip of the prairie; lamps and lanterns were being lighted, and there was the familiar smell of woodsmoke in the air. Jeff's lonesomeness and discontent thrived in the gathering dusk.

He stood in front of the Paradise for a while, watching a group of Snake hands ride whooping in from the north. Jeff envied them their gaiety, the sense of freedom that was always with them. When he first left the Sewell house he had thought to get on as a cowhand with one of the big outfits, as Nathan had done so long ago. But the common hand's pay of six bits a day and chuck did not appeal to him — he had learned quickly that he could do much better at Surratt's gambling tables.

But his boyhood notion of the cowhand's life was strong within him, and he could still smile at their loud talk, their vanity and swagger. He noted that some of the hands were no older than himself, eighteen or nineteen at the most. In this country they were not looked upon as boys.

The cowhands disappeared into the new Green House saloon, and Jeff lingered for a few minutes longer in front of the Paradise. The pungent smell of woodsmoke brought back memories. On the slope to the east of town he could see the straggling barefoot "cowboys" bringing in the family cows. Not long ago he had been one of them, a tow-headed kid with hardly a care in the world.

The sight of Wirt Sewell on the other side of the street brought his bitterness into sharp focus. Coming out of Baxter's store, Wirt looked old and somehow shrunken, but he wrung no pity from Jeff Blaine. The very sight of Wirt could send him into a rage, and now Jeff turned stiffly and faced in the other direction so he wouldn't have to look at him.

Jeff had heard with bitter pleasure how Wirt's tin shop was going to ruin. That was the town's way of punishing Beulah for making a fool of it. Even the grangers were canceling their orders, sending all the way to Landow for their windmills and water tanks and tin piping. They said it was only a matter of time before he went broke and would be forced to leave Plainsville;

they said he spent his days piddling with buckets and tubs which nobody would buy.

Not until it was too late to escape did Jeff realize that Wirt had crossed the street and was coming toward him. He felt something inside him go cold and hard as Wirt said, "Jeff, won't you talk to me?"

Jeff turned angrily and faced a sagging, defeated shadow of a man. He said tightly, "We have nothing to talk about."

"Jeff, can't you ever forgive us?"

He said shortly, "No!"

Wirt's face was flabby and blank. "I didn't think you would. But I had to ask. I'm not standing up for what Beulah did — it was a terrible thing. It was wrong — she knows it now — but at the time she thought it was the best thing for you. That's why she did it, Jeff."

Jeff laughed harshly. "Is that what she's telling people?"

Wirt shrugged wearily. "She tells them nothing. She hasn't seen anybody since you left us. She won't talk — not even to me." Nervously, he wiped the back of his hand across his mouth. "Your Aunt Beulah's sick, Jeff. She's shut herself up as if she was dead and that house was her tomb. If you'd just go over and see her —"

"But I won't," Jeff said cruelly. "One day my pa will come back to Plainsville, and if he wants to forgive her, that's his business. But I never will!"

Wirt shrunk before the hate in Jeff's eyes. His head dropped, and after a moment he shuffled back across the street.

Jeff felt his nerves quiver. He turned on his heel and walked stiffly toward Bert Surratt's.

It was a quiet night in Surratt's saloon, everything considered. The saloonkeeper leaned on the bar, idly watching two Cross 4 hands have a fling at the wheel of fortune. The excitement over the shooting that afternoon had died down. Every hour or so someone came in to report on Phil Costain, who was still in Doc Shipley's sick room. There was nothing much to do except wait for the marshal to come back with Somerson. Bert Surratt smiled faintly; that's when the excitement would begin.

Old Seth Lewellen, leaning heavily on an oak root cane, shouldered through the swinging doors. "You hear about Costain?" he asked Surratt. "Doc Shipley says he'll pull through. Takes more'n bullets to kill a drayman, it looks like."

Bert nodded. "Phil's a tough one," he agreed.

The old man waited expectantly, hoping the news would bring a round on the house. When Bert made no move, Lewellen went out again, mumbling to himself.

Surratt yawned. Mac Butler, the blacksmith, and Forrest Slater were playing low-stake stud with a pair of grangers. Two men from Big Hat nursed their drinks at the far end of the bar. A slow night.

The new saloon down the street, the Green House, had taken part of the cowhand business, but Bert wasn't worried. When things were lively there was plenty of business to go around. Then the batwings swung open and Jeff Blaine came in.

Blaine nodded at a whisky bottle and the saloonkeeper slid it up the bar, a glass after it. Jeff poured one and could not control the shudder that went through him as he downed it.

Pretending to watch the wheel of fortune, Surratt studied Jeff from the corner of his eye. He didn't like the boy any better than he had liked his pa — they both carried the smell of trouble about them. Anyway, Bert had little use for fuzz-faced kids who toted guns and tried to act like men. He didn't like selling them whisky, either, but what could you do when that was your business? One of these strutting kids could give you more trouble than the whole Cross 4 after roundup.

But there was something about that tense face and those angry eyes that made a man think before he started something with Jeff Blaine, even if he was just a kid. That second-hand Colt's could kill you just as dead as a man's gun.

Now Surratt turned his gaze frankly on the kid. "Hear about Costain?" he asked tentatively.

Jeff nodded shortly, but said nothing.

Bert slid a new bottle down to the Big Hat men at the other end of the bar. For a moment he focused his attention on the stud game, but there was little there to interest him. He mopped the bar and continued his silent study of the Blaine boy.

At the moment Jeff turned his attention to the stud game. It was about his size; he was smart enough not to get in with professionals. But the anger that came with talking to Wirt was still in him, and he knew that he was in no condition to study cards.

Then they heard the horses enter the far end of the street. Surratt cocked his head with interest.

"Maybe that is Elec's posse coming back with Somerson," he commented.

Jeff didn't care who it was. His nerves were taut; he felt at loose ends and all alone. He poured another glass of fiery whisky, hating the green taste of it but swallowing it in the hope that it would relax him.

Now they heard the tramp of boots on the plank walk outside the saloon. Jeff turned and saw Elec Blasingame and his deputy standing in the doorway, the other members of the posse behind them. Kirk Logan's face was drawn with anger, but the marshal himself was the picture of rage.

All eyes in the saloon were focused on the dirty, sweat-stained men in the doorway. The saloonkeeper cleared his throat uneasily. "You find Somerson, Marshal?"

Blasingame made no show of hearing. He came into the room, his anger directed at Jeff. The marshal was no longer young; he had grown fat and he was not as quick as he had once been, but he was still regarded as the most dangerous man in Plainsville. And he had never looked more dangerous than he did at this moment.

Instinctively, Bert Surratt backed away from the bar. The Big Hat men downed their drinks and drifted toward the far wall. Jeff stayed where he was, watching Elec and the deputy, prepared for whatever was to come. He abandoned all caution. His nervous tension and frustration suddenly became an urge for violence.

He set his whisky glass on the bar. "You looking for me, Marshal?"

Kirk Logan made an ugly sound and started to move in. The marshal stopped him with an outstretched arm. "Stay out of it, Kirk!" He turned to Jeff, his voice hoarse. "Are you proud of yourself, Blaine? Thanks to you, a killer got away free!"

Jeff was surprised, exhilarated at the confidence that had taken control of him. He said coolly, "I don't know what you're talking about, Elec."

"You know, all right!" the marshal snarled. "That rider you saw — you knew he was headin' west, not east."

Jeff shot a glance around the room, but said nothing.

"Don't waste your breath on him," Kirk Logan growled.

Jeff wheeled on the deputy. "Maybe you've got some ideas of your own you'd like to try!"

"That's enough!" Elec snapped, holding his deputy at bay with angry eyes. His fat jowls shook as he wheeled on Jeff. "Son, you better take that chip off your shoulder," he said with forced calm. "You keep looking for trouble hard enough and you're bound to find it — more than you can handle, maybe."

"I'll take my chances," Jeff said coldly.

Elec's anger got away from him. A big clawlike hand shot out and grabbed the front of Jeff's shirt. Before the action was half completed, Jeff grabbed his Colt's and rammed the muzzle hard into Blasingame's soft belly.

Jeff felt every muscle in his body quiver, every nerve taut and singing. He watched grayness replace the flush of anger in the marshal's face. Jeff Blaine had never known an excitement so intense; he had never dreamed of such power as he held in his own right hand at that moment.

If there was ever a doubt as to whether Jeff Blaine could handle a gun, it had now vanished. Even Kirk Logan, in his amazement, lost the keen edge of his anger. Bert Surratt's breath whistled between his teeth as he waited tensely.

Slowly, very slowly, the tension began to relax.

Jeff heard his own voice saying, "Turn loose of me, Elec. Don't ever touch me again."

Very carefully the marshal withdrew his hand. He stood perfectly still, recovering from his first shock, as Jeff shot the revolver back into its holster. The silence in the room was as hard as steel.

At last Elec Blasingame shook his head. "I shouldn't have grabbed you like that. But if you ever take another notion to throw down on me, be sure you pull the trigger. Next time I'll know what to expect." He nodded stiffly to Logan and the two of them turned toward the door.

CHAPTER FOURTEEN

It was a busy day, as all Saturdays were in Plainsville. Wirt Sewell stood outside his tin shop, a forlorn, faded figure of a man, gazing vacantly at the mill of farm wagons and saddle animals in the street. Solemn farmers, their faces raw from recent shaves, gathered in the stores and on the streets to talk crops; farm women gossiped in the stores or near the wagons in the wide alley behind Main Street.

Impatient cowhands lined up for haircuts and shaves and baths at the barber shops, looking forward to whisky at the Green House or Bert Surratt's, and gambling, and maybe a woman. Some of them, the ones sober enough to pass inspection, would stay over for the Masonic dance. By noon the street became so clotted with wagons and hacks and horses and oxen as to become impassable.

On that day Plainsville took on the aspect of a farming town, grangers outnumbering cowhands three to one. All the stores were busy, clerks run ragged; tempers flared, but it was all a part of the day and no one would have missed it. Cowhands prowled the sidewalks and haunted the saloons, arrogant as always, staying aloof and to themselves. Elec Blasingame and his deputies were kept busy settling arguments, stopping fights, trying to clear the street for traffic.

Not long ago Wirt Sewell had enjoyed these days of excitement and clamor; he had felt a part of it. Once he had had more orders than he and Jeff could fill — now there was not enough business to keep only himself busy. Only the tin shop, of all the stores in Plainsville, was empty of customers.

But Wirt no longer worried about the shop. He could think only of his wife, and of Jeff.

He told himself that he was still a young man with many good years left before him, but he felt old and empty. He listened for a moment to the bawling from the cattle pens, and then realized that people were watching him. An old man warming himself in the sun, he thought. He went back into his empty shop.

From his window he saw Amy Wintworth and her mother going into Baxter's store. He smiled faintly, unable to understand how everything had gone so wrong so fast. He had thought about it until his head swam, but there seemed to be no answer. All Beulah's regrets couldn't undo the damage she had caused.

Things will never be the same again, he thought hopelessly. Beulah and I might as well get used to it.

Then he saw Amy come out of Baxter's. The beginning of a new idea began working in Wirt's mind as he watched her pick her way across the dusty street. On impulse, he hurried back to the sidewalk and called to her.

"Amy! Can I talk to you a minute?"

Surprise was in her eyes, but not the disgust that he had seen so often in others. Wirt took her hand and helped her up to the walk.

They found privacy inside the shop. "Amy," he said awkwardly, "how long has it been since you saw Jeff?"

She dropped her glance. "Yesterday, Mr. Sewell. We went out to Stone Ridge."

"Yes," Wirt said heavily. "I heard he had some land out there. Did he — say anything about his aunt?" Sudden color appeared in her cheeks, and Wirt murmured, "Yes, I guess he did." Then he steeled himself and asked bluntly, "Amy, do you love him?"

She looked up quickly, startled. But when she saw the gray weariness in his face, she felt more at ease.

"I don't know, Mr. Sewell. I used to be so sure of everything, but now — My father has forbidden me to see him again."

Wirt said quietly, "I guess I can't blame Ford for that." He moved a hand aimlessly over his face, forcing a smile. "Well, thank you for stopping, Amy."

Wirt turned slightly, gazing emptily at the dust clouds that rose over the cattle pens. "It's a funny thing," he said, "but I guess Beulah and I didn't know how much the boy meant to us until he went away. Or maybe Beulah did know — because she did that thing for what she thought was his own good. Amy, does he hate us as much as he thinks he does?"

Her silence was her answer.

Wirt sighed. "Well, I guess he has the right to hate. But so did Nathan, long ago, when he was Jeff's age. Jeff's pa wasn't a bad boy at all. Oh, Nathan was a little wild, maybe, but a hard worker and not really bad. He worked in the stables before your own pa came to Plainsville; made his own living and took some hard knocks while doing it. So Nate was bitter on this town, like Jeff is now. He married Beulah's baby sister, but his wife died that first winter. Pneumonia, right after the boy was born. Nate blamed it on the town, because it wouldn't trust him for money to buy medicine and rations."

Now Wirt turned from the window and faced Amy. "I guess I'm scared," he said evenly. "I watched Nate's anger grow to a thing of destruction, just the way Jeff's is growing now. I saw the violence mount in Nate until there was no holding him, until he was bound to kill somebody before he was through." Slowly he shook his head. "Amy, I am scared. I can see it happening all over again in Jeff, and there's nothing I can do to stop it. I think Nate saw it in his son, too, and was scared by it."

Amy stood as straight as a lance, her face pale. "Mr. Sewell, is there anything I can do?"

"No — not if you don't love him."

"I didn't say that."

Wirt smiled faintly and nodded. "I know. But Ford Wintworth can be a strong-willed man when he's riled. I guess he's heard that Jeff threw down on the marshal last night."

"I can handle my father," Amy said firmly.

Heat had driven Jeff from his hot, boxlike room above Frank Ludlow's store. For a moment he stood on the plank walk at the foot of the stairs, amazed how alone a person could feel with people swarming all around him. His anger from the night before had subsided, and there was nothing to replace it.

He was sluggish from a sleepless night, and that unreal feeling of hollowness was growing again within him.

As he stood there he caught the sidelong glances thrown in his direction. There was new respect, even fear, in those glances. Here was the man who had made Elec Blasingame back down. Here was a dangerous man, even though he looked like a kid. With elaborate unconcern, grangers, cowhands, and townspeople sidestepped when they approached him, careful not to jostle him.

Jeff smiled faintly and without humor. Without firing a shot he had suddenly acquired a reputation as a dangerous gunman. The name of Blaine had made it so, at one quick impulsive draw on the marshal.

For a long time they had wondered. For a long time they had considered his arrogance, quietly pondering the question of whether Nate Blaine's violent blood actually flowed in his son's veins. Now they knew, or they thought they did.

Only Jeff and Elec Blasingame knew that the show of deadliness had been mostly luck, because Elec had not been prepared for the draw. Ignoring such an obvious truth would be suicide, and Jeff instinctively knew it. What would happen another time, with Elec ready for him, he could not say; he hoped he'd never have to find out.

Only after it was over, in the thoughtful hours of a restless night, had he realized how close he had come to killing a man. This was something that he had not considered until now, and the thought was terrifying.

Ralph Striker was in the Paradise when Jeff came in for breakfast. The lawman threw him a quick, hard glance. Then, with faked good humor, Striker walked down to Jeff's end of the counter. "Morning, Blaine," he said casually, helping himself to several toothpicks.

Jeff nodded.

"Do me a favor, will you?" the deputy asked, his thin smile a bit forced. "Try to stay out of trouble. I'd like to get in a full day's sleep for a change."

Jeff frowned as Striker got his hat and went out. Not until later did he learn the meaning behind the deputy's quiet warning.

Out of the Paradise, Jeff fingered the few bills and loose silver in his pocket. Because of that piece of land, he had almost tricked himself into thinking that he was a successful gambler, but those few dollars that made up his bankroll proved otherwise. He did not have the experience to sit in on high stake games, and dollars came slow and hard from the cautious store clerks and farmers. He had been able to hold off the urge to plunge, but now he felt impatience gnawing at him.

If he only had a stake, he thought, he could stock his land and have the beginning of a brand of his own. One thing he had learned — gambling as seen from a felted table in Bert Surratt's wasn't as exciting as he had imagined. Also, he remembered the way Amy's eyes had lighted up when she had looked down on that valley of grass.

But you need more than land to make a place pay. He could not go to Amy and say, "Come with me, Amy, and we'll live in the squatter's broken-down shack, and maybe the bank will loan us enough to get started on."

The bank hadn't helped Nathan Blaine when he had needed it, and it wouldn't help his son. A man needed a stake before he could go to a girl like Amy, before he could face the fierce rejection in Ford Wintworth's eyes.

Frowning, he walked into Bert Surratt's, raked the crowded bar with a practiced glance, and studied the tables and the men playing at them. To get what he wants, a man has to take a chance, he told himself.

He moved back to where a crowd of idlers stood watching the play at one table. Jeff studied the litter of silver, gold, and a few greenbacks on the table and thought, With a little luck a man could stock a good-sized range out of a game like this. He moved forward, noting how the idlers split away from him.

"Room for one more?"

Chet Blakely, Snake range boss, looked up coldly. "This is no game for boys."

It was a cold, seasoned bunch at the table. Blakely, who had won and lost outfits of his own in his time; Bus Cheetham, who could gamble for a living with the best of them if he didn't own a piece of the Cross 4 where he worked as foreman. Besides the two cattlemen, there was a railroad man from Landow; Brad Littlefield, the stage agent; and two hands from

Big Hat who were pushing strings of luck. All of them looked up, smiling thinly at Blakely's small joke.

Jeff felt his face grow warm. "Do you want another player, or don't you?" he asked.

"He's old enough to tote a gun," Bus Cheetham drawled; "he's old enough to lose his money. Sit in, Blaine; we'll see how much Nate taught you about the game."

It did not take Jeff long to learn that it had not been enough.

With appalling efficiency they took his cash and then began taking great bites at the two sections that he had won less than two days before. And soon it was gone — all gone.

Jeff felt shaken and weak. He had planned so boldly, and now he had nothing. He owned less than he had the day he had hurled curses at Wirt and Beulah Sewell and turned his back on their house. A few pieces of clothing, he thought angrily, a second-hand Colt's — that's what I've got. Not even a horse and rig!

Chet Blakely grinned as Jeff signed over the deed to the land. "Here, kid," he said harshly, "don't say we tried to clean you." He flipped a gold double eagle at him.

Only then did anger come. Jeff kicked his chair back, grabbed the edge of the table and shoved. The amazed range boss caught the table in his lap and fell back. He sprawled on the floor, showered with money and cards.

"You can keep your money!" Jeff said tightly.

"God damn you!" Blakely snarled. With a savage swipe of his arm he brushed money from his chest and sprang to his feet. He rushed blindly but Jeff kicked the table in his way and Blakely sprawled again.

Once more he got up, raging, big and ugly as a bull buffalo. Within the range boss's two big arms was enough strength to break a man in half, and that was his intent as he rushed again.

But this time something stopped him. The fire in Jeff Blaine's eyes, the pale gray line of his tightly compressed mouth. Blakely saw that right hand cupped at the hip, ready to grab, and he sensed the violence that was ready to burst. He stopped. He had the good sense to realize that size and strength were no advantages. Colonel Colt's deadly two pounds of steel had equalized all that — victory went to the quick and eager.

Chet Blakely was quick enough for a man his size, but he was not eager. He had laughed about Elec Blasingame letting a punk kid throw down on him, but he wasn't laughing now. He made no move toward his own revolver. Instead, he held his hand well away from his side.

It was clear to all in the room that Chet was buffaloed. The range boss was not going to be the first to test the untried speed of a wild kid's draw; he gambled only with money. Nor did any other man in the saloon seem anxious to try his hand.

At last Blakely forced an uneasy laugh. "Relax, kid. I'm not going to hurt you."

"I know," Jeff said coldly.

Chet swallowed. "You lost that land fair and square."

"I'm not saying I didn't."

Then something happened in Blakely's eyes. It was the quick but cautious look of a wolf, and Jeff studied it. Too late did he realize that someone had got behind him.

He jumped as a cold, hard muzzle jammed into the small of his back, and at the same time a voice said: "Hold your hands in front of you."

It was Elec Blasingame.

The suddenness of the action left Jeff stunned. Elec said mildly, "You've got a lot to learn, boy; Nate never would have let a man get behind him by the back door. Now drop your gun."

The gray shade of death had slipped from Chet Blakely's face, and now he gloated. "Marshal, that kill-crazy kid ought to be run out of town!"

Elec glanced at him. "Has he killed somebody?"

"No, but —"

"Then," the marshal said gently, "I guess I'll handle it my own way. Drop the gun, son."

Jeff was surprised to discover his mind working with the clean, polished precision of a fine watch. Instantly, he remembered the "spin" that Nathan had shown him so long ago, that miraculous trick of reversing a pistol in your hand while seeming to hand it over butt first.

But Elec was not to be caught off guard this time. He increased the pressure slightly, pressing the muzzle a bit harder in Jeff's back.

"Don't bother handing it to me," he said dryly. "Just slip the buckle." The marshal took the revolver. "All right — march."

"I didn't do anything. You can't lock me up."

"I can. And I will," Elec said flatly.

There was nothing to do. With a gun in his back, Jeff focused his hate on Chet Blakely, as though to warn him the fight wasn't over. Then he shrugged and walked stiffly out of the saloon.

The marshal put him in the cell with two drunk cowhands and locked the door. Jeff grabbed the bars and glared. "You'll be sorry for this, Elec!"

The marshal sighed heavily and shook his head. "I just don't know what to do with you, Blaine, and that's the gospel truth. Can't you see you're not hurting anybody but yourself?"

"I figure that's my business."

"Not when you go on the prod. Then it gets to be my business. Do you know what's going to happen if you don't take that chip off your shoulder? You'll end up like your pa; you'll let your hate get you in so deep that you'll never be able to get out. One of these days some drunk cowhand'll get the notion he's a gunfighter and force you to show your hand."

"I can take care of myself."

Blasingame smiled bitterly. "So could Nate, but what did it prove? Your pa's a wanted killer. With telegraph wire strung all over the Southwest, he doesn't dare come back to his own country, to the place where he was born and raised, not even to see his son."

"My pa will come back when he gets ready."

The marshal nodded. "Maybe. But it'll be the last trip he'll ever take. The law will be waiting for him." He turned and walked heavily back to his office . . .

It was midafternoon when Amy Wintworth came to the office to see him. Elec touched his hatbrim with a forced smile. "Come in, Amy. It's not often we get such pretty visitors down here."

Amy could offer no smile in return. "I heard that Jeff was —"

"Locked up," the marshal finished for her. "A little to-do over at Bert's place. Nothing serious."

"But serious enough to lock him up."

Blasingame looked at her, saw the urgency behind her eyes. "Yes," he said slowly, "I guess it was. Have a chair, Amy." He waited until she was seated.

"May I see him?" she asked.

"I don't think it would be wise; he's pretty worked up. What did you want to see him about?"

"I want to ask him to make up with his Aunt Beulah," Amy said tightly.

Elec whistled softly in surprise. "I don't think he'd ever do that, Amy. He hates Beulah Sewell as much as I ever saw one person hate another. That's the seat of all his trouble, I think — he's so full of hate that it spills over onto everybody he crosses."

"Marshal, have you seen Beulah Sewell recently?"

He frowned faintly. "No, I don't think so. Not since —"

"Not since the town learned Nathan wasn't the one who killed Jeff Harper and robbed the bank? No one has seen her since then except Wirt, and me. I just came from the Sewell house."

Amy closed her eyes for a moment, her thoughts flying back to that bleak little house, locked and sealed and quiet as a tomb. She said slowly, "I don't think you'd know her, Marshal. She's as unreal as a corpse; she hates herself more than Jeff ever could."

Elec rubbed his face thoughtfully. "I guess I haven't thought much about Beulah except to despise her for what she did. Like everybody else." Gazing up at the ceiling, he smiled thinly. "It's a funny thing. You can fight with a man, or steal from him, or even shoot him, and the chances are pretty good that he'll forgive you if you give him a chance. But prove a man a fool and he'll hate you all his life. That's what Beulah did. We all swallowed that lie of hers, and then looked like fools when the truth came out."

"But," Amy asked, "don't you think it would be a better town if people would forgive her?"

"Sure," Elec shrugged, "but it's a big order. Especially for Jeff."

"Impossible?"

"Just not very likely, let's say."

She sat straight, her mouth compressed to a grim, determined line. One moment she had all the poise and steel of a queen, and the next moment she was a frightened young woman, sobbing.

Elec moved uneasily. "Now, now, Amy, there's no use in that." He tugged at a red handkerchief in his hip pocket and handed it to her across the desk.

"I'm sorry. That was a foolish thing to do," she said.

"You like the boy, don't you, Amy?"

She nodded. "But not the way he's going. Not what I see for him in the future. Sometimes I see so much of Nathan in him that it frightens me."

Elec nodded, knowing what she meant. It wasn't Jeff's blood that made him act the way he did, it was that element of pure tragedy — circumstance. The same kind of circumstance that had made Nate the kind of man he now was.

Few persons ever thought of the marshal as a sensitive man, but now he felt a vague horror growing within him as he considered what violence circumstance could build. How could you fight a thing as irrevocable as fate? How could you change the direction of destiny?

People saw Elec Blasingame as a logical, plodding man whose job it was to hunt down, capture, or kill those who ran off the one-way track of conventional standards. Few guessed that he was often filled with rage and futility, as he was now, because he was helpless to change the inevitable. In his job there were no human switches to be thrown, no means of sidetracking passion, or hate, or anger. His job was to wait patiently and then shoot down those who left the rails.

Elec sat heavily behind his desk, his big fists knotted. He had been in this job long enough; he felt old, he had lost his zest for the work. He knew from experience that it was only a matter of time, and not much of that, before Jeff Blaine left the rails. The job of stopping the boy would be his, and he did not relish it.

Several seconds had passed since she had spoken, and now Amy said quietly, "May I see him, Marshal?"

"Now?"

She nodded, and there was a finality to the gesture that Elec could feel to his bones. "You have the right, if that's what you want. Are you going to ask him to make up with his aunt?"

"It's the only chance he has, isn't it? If there's no forgiveness in him, I might as well know it now."

"And if he won't listen?" Elec asked.

There was no need of an answer.

It was well past midnight when the cell became so filled with drunk cowhands that Elec let Jeff go.

"Go to bed," the marshal said. "I have all the trouble I need tonight."

"I'll take my gun before I go," Jeff said icily.

Sighing, the marshal took the Colt's from the desk drawer. "I don't suppose you had sense enough to listen to Amy when she tried to talk to you this afternoon."

Jeff glared and did not answer. He buckled the cartridge belt around his waist, turned stiffly on his heel, and headed up the stairs.

The air outside was clean and sweet, and he dragged deep gulps of it into his lungs when he reached the side-walk. All around him were the Saturday night sounds of a western town. The clang of the Green House piano, the sound of bawdy laughter from the Paradise and Surratt's. Above him, fiddles sang in the Masonic hall, and the building trembled with the heavy tramping of country dancing. Jeff wondered bitterly if Amy was up there — she often came with Todd when Jeff was busy or had forgotten to ask her.

He headed toward the outside stairs and gazed angrily up at the splash of lamplight on the landing. His pockets were empty; he did not have the door price, even if he had wanted to go. He turned and walked quickly away.

He hated the thought of going back to the blistering heat of his room, but there was nowhere else to go. And he had to think, he had to plan. The stench of the jail cell was still in his nostrils and his anger was a hard knot in the pit of his stomach.

Crossing the street, he gazed into the night and ached to break away from this place that he hated, and which hated him. He longed to escape, as his pa had done, and yet he knew that he couldn't leave.

More than a lack of money kept him here. His craving for vengeance was strong — but even more important, there was Amy. This was the second time that she had seen him behind bars, and that knowledge angered him. As always, she had asked the impossible of him, wanting him to make up with Beulah. He would have taken a thing so unthinkable as a joke if he had not glimpsed that blank look of finality in her face. He tried to put it from his mind, telling himself she would get over it. But this time he could not be sure. Uncertainty gnawed at his nerves. He had never seen her look at him the way she had looked today. It was as though shutters had been drawn behind her eyes; that she had erected an invisible, impenetrable wall between them.

She had said quietly, "I'm sorry, Jeff," and turned away from him and left. It had never been that way before, no matter how angry she got, and the memory of how she had looked and sounded set his nerves to jumping.

He did not see the stranger until he had almost reached the outside stairs at the side of Ludlow's store. A tall, big-boned man in his late thirties, he loafed quietly in the darkness under the wooden awning. Jeff gave him only a brief glance, took him for a drifter, and turned toward the stairs.

"Blaine?" the man asked quietly.

Surprised, Jeff turned toward him. "Yes?"

"Then you're Nate Blaine's kid. I'm a friend of your pa's."

CHAPTER FIFTEEN

The stranger left the shadows, and Jeff noted the big sunburst rowels of his Mexican spurs. He was trail-dirty and shabby, his stubbled face partly hidden under the dark overhang of his shapeless hat. "So you're Nate Blaine's kid," he said again, and laughed shortly. "I saw the to-do in the saloon today. I take it that fat marshal ain't a special friend of yours."

"What about my pa?" Jeff said bluntly. "You said you knew him."

"Sure, we hired out to the same bunch in Mexico for a while."

"Is he still down there?"

The stranger shrugged. "Far as I know. My friend can tell you all about it; he just came from Mexico."

Jeff frowned. "Who's your friend?"

A match suddenly blazed in the stranger's hand. He held the flame to the end of a thin cigarette and shot the matchstick into the street. "He's your friend, too, kid," he said. "You saved his neck yesterday when you turned that posse off his trail."

Amazement was in Jeff's voice. "Bill Somerson? The one that shot Costain?"

Smiling thinly, the tall stranger nodded. "He's got a message for you — from your pa."

Jeff shot quick glances up and down the street. "Maybe we'd better go somewhere else to talk."

The man shook his head. "I've got nothin' else to say. Somerson does his own talkin'. If you want that message from your pa, you'd better hightail it down south. Do you know where Rifle Creek forks with Little River, across the county line? About a mile north of the fork there's a shack, and that's where Somerson's waitin' for you."

Jeff shook his head, not in rejection of the proposition, but because it was hard to believe. "Can't you give me an idea what the message is about?"

"Just that it's important; that's all Somerson would tell me. Straight from Nate Blaine to his kid, he said. Bill's kind of taken a personal interest in the matter, I guess, after the way you steered the posse off him. Have you got a horse?"

When Jeff shook his head, the stranger laughed. "I guessed as much, seein' the way they cleaned you in that stud game. Take that claybank at the rack; it's mine. If I have any ridin' to do, I can hire one at the stables."

Jeff looked closely at the stranger, seeing hardness in the bony face, a kind of brutal humor in the pale eyes. As the man talked, Jeff instinctively tensed up, not liking what he saw. He didn't trust the stranger's words any more than he trusted his smile.

Jeff said bluntly, "It seems like you're going pretty far out of your way to do me a favor. Why?"

The smile disappeared; blankness took its place. "I told you Somerson wants to talk to you, kid. If you don't want to know what your pa has to say, then I'll go back to where I come from."

"Wait a minute," Jeff said quickly, knowing that he had to go. He had to know what message Nathan had sent that was so important. "A mile north of the fork. All right, I'll go."

The stranger nodded shortly. "Be careful nobody trails you. I'll take the claybank around to the alley and you can take it from there." Jeff stood in the shadows as the man went to the horse and rode lazily around the corner of the bank building. Jeff felt that hand of caution firmly upon his shoulder; a vague uncertainty nagged at him as rider and horse disappeared into the darkness of the alley.

Common sense told him that a wanted man like Somerson would not expose himself simply to relay a message for a friend. And this tall stranger was branded a hard-case in every move he made. Still, five long years had passed since he had had direct word from Nathan. He was sick of the town and would be glad enough to put it behind him for a while. He headed for the alley.

"Remember to cover your trail," the stranger reminded him, as Jeff stepped up to the saddle. "The name's Milan Fay," the tall man added as Jeff was riding away. "Somerson will want to be sure who sent you."

As he rode to the south, the lights of the town grew small, the singing of fiddles became threadlike whispers of sound, the laughter of drunken cowhands dissolved in the night. Soon the town and its sounds had disappeared and a blanket of silence enveloped the prairie.

A vague uneasiness mounted within him as he rode deeper into the darkness.

But in the bigness of the night, details did not seem important, and he soon put uncertainty behind him and rode at ease. Nathan had not forgotten him — that was the important thing. Nathan's strong hand could still reach him and comfort him, even from Mexico.

Jeff could almost imagine that Nate himself was waiting for him somewhere to the south, in the darkness, and he urged the claybank to a quicker gait. He let himself smile as he remembered Nathan throwing back his head, holding the world at bay with the violence in his eyes — and for a little while he forgot to be angry and loosened the band of hate that squeezed his brain.

It was almost sunup when Jeff approached the forks. The lip of the eastern prairie seemed etched in blood and the sky became a skillful blend of brilliant blues and subtle grays. Suddenly a great orange sun appeared and the prairie blazed as though with fire.

In this new light Jeff paused for a moment and studied his backtrail; then he nudged the claybank through a thicket of salt cedar, crossed the dry bed of Little River and headed north.

This was a raw, red country of eroded clay and dwarfed trees and sage, as barren as the floor of a dried ocean. Not many men would pass this way, not even drifters.

Soon Jeff saw the weathered outline of an abandoned shack, a sorry affair of sod and scrub oak logs with the roof half gone, the chimney crumbling. Cautiously now, he eased the claybank forward. Suddenly the doorway of the shack was filled with the thick-set form of a man.

"Somerson?" Jeff called.

"Who wants to know?"

"Jefferson Blaine. Nate Blaine's my father."

Somerson stepped through the doorway, a snub-nosed carbine on his hip at the ready. "Who sent you?"

"A man called Fay. Milan Fay."

Somerson laughed and slung the carbine in the crook of his arm. "I would of knowed you anyway, kid; you've got the Blaine mark stamped all over you. Tie your animal to a brush and climb down."

Somerson waited by the corner of the shack as Jeff left the claybank in a thicket of blackjack. He held out a big hand as Jeff came up to him. "By hell, you're Nate all over again. I'm proud to shake hands with you, son; that business of turnin' the posse just about saved this dirty neck of mine!"

Jeff studied the man quietly, his hand smothered in Somerson's bearlike fist. "I didn't know who they were after," he said.

Somerson laughed again. "No matter. It showed clear enough whose side you're on, and that's good enough for Bill Somerson. Yes sir, you're Nate Blaine all over again. Come on in and we'll have breakfast."

Somerson turned abruptly and lunged back through the doorway. Jeff followed him inside and was hit by the pungent smell of frying salt pork. The shack itself had the powdery smell of bleached bones about it; the dirt floor had grown up in weeds which had been tramped down. A small smokeless fire of carefully selected hardwood was going in the fireplace, where fat pork sizzled in an iron skillet.

Jeff turned his attention on Somerson, who was turning the meat with the point of his pocket knife. He saw a florid man in his early forties, bulging and heavy with hard fat; his long, pale hair was as fine as silk, flowing and drifting about his head with every slight breeze within the shack.

Jeff squatted beside the fireplace, putting his back against the sod wall. "The man called Fay said you had a message for me."

"That's right." Somerson opened a can of hardtack and dumped the rocklike biscuits onto a saddle blanket. From a scant store of provisions in the corner of the shack, he found some coffee. "Me and Nate rode for the same bunch down in Chihuahua. When he heard I was headed back this way, he wanted me to look you up." He poured coffee into the hardtack can and added water from a canteen. "This ain't much of a way to live," he said blandly, putting the can on the fire to boil. "But I figure to do better before long. Is that fat marshal still lookin' for me?"

"Elec Blasingame doesn't give up easily."

The outlaw laughed. "He'll never find me here. Wouldn't do him any good if he did; I'm out of his county."

"I wouldn't count too much on that," Jeff said. "Elec's just a town marshal; doesn't have any legal authority outside the limits of Plainsville. But that didn't stop him from bringing a posse after you before."

Somerson frowned. "I thought you didn't like lawdogs."

"I don't, but it would be a mistake not to give Elec his due. Once he gets his teeth into something, he's hard to break loose."

Somerson rubbed his chin thoughtfully. "That might be a good thing to know. But I was talkin' about your pa, not the marshal." He busied himself with the pork, not looking at Jeff. "I guess you know Nate had a little trouble over in the New Mexico country. He's got an idea the government marshal would like to get his hands on him; that's why he's stickin' below the Border. Your pa'd like to see you, son."

Jeff felt his heart hammering. "When?"

"Pretty soon, I guess. I can take you south when the time comes — but first Nate wants you to do him a favor — a big one." Somerson set the skillet off the fire, and now he turned his eyes directly on Jeff. "I'll tell you the truth, kid. Your pa's pretty hot about the way they tried to railroad him in this town. He said he wants you to settle the score for him. Nate Blaine wants that town of yours turned upside down and shook till its teeth rattles. You understand?"

Jeff heard his own breath whistle between his teeth. It didn't sound like Nate, putting his work on somebody else. "He said that?"

Somerson stared at him. "Would I have a reason to lie to you?"

"No. I guess not."

"And hasn't Nate got plenty of right to his hate?"

"Yes. Both of us have."

"Now you sound like your pa!" the outlaw grinned. He speared a piece of fat pork with his knife, clamped it between two pieces of hardtack and began eating. "Help yourself," he said, nodding. "You know, I rode a long piece out of my way just to see you, kid. But I told Nate I'd look you up, and I don't go back on my word."

"You still haven't given me the message."

"Don't be in such a hurry; I'm just gettin' to it. We'll have to go back a way to get at the beginning. Me and Nate were ridin' together for this reb general on the other side of the Border, and that's how I came to find out how they railroaded him up here."

"He told you?"

"That, and plenty more. The more he thought about it the madder he got, I guess, and a man like Nate can get pretty mad in five years' time. Now, it was a bank job they tried to stick him with, wasn't it?"

"And murder."

"The banker — I almost forgot about him. Anyway, down there in Mexico, Nate stews about it, and after a while he gets to thinkin' what a hell of a thing it would be if he could come back here and really rob that bank. Of course, what with telegraph wires strung all over Texas these days, he couldn't show his face up here. That's where you come in kid. Are you beginnin' to see the way Nate figured it out?"

Jeff stared. "He wants *me* to rob the bank?"

Somerson's laughter was a sudden outburst that was over almost as soon as it started. "You're gettin' the idea, kid, but it's not as risky as you make it sound. I'm here to help you."

Jeff glared at the outlaw in disbelief. His memory went back five years, and again he saw the way Nathan had looked at him from behind the bars of Blasingame's jail. At a time like that, when he could have drenched his son with his own hate, Nathan had chosen to tell him nothing. Nathan had let him walk away hating him, because he had thought it would be better for the boy that way.

It didn't stand to reason for that kind of man to ask the things that Somerson claimed for him. Slowly, stiffly, Jeff got to his feet.

"What's the matter?" The outlaw frowned.

"I guess I'll head back for Plainsville."

Somerson folded his pocket knife, and Jeff could almost see the thoughts racing behind his eyes. At last he slipped the knife into his pocket and rose to his feet, surprising Jeff with a mild grin.

"I didn't fool you, did I? Well, I should have known better than to try to fool a kid of Nate Blaine's."

"He never said anything about that bank, did he?" Jeff asked tightly.

Somerson shook his head, as though in wonder. "You're just like Nate, all right. Want to see all the cards on the table, don't you? I'll give it to you straight, kid. Nate never sent me up here to look you up, and he never said he wanted you to rob a bank for him. I made that up out of my head, but the rest is the truth. The way he hates this town of yours, especially. Sometimes I thought he was goin' to come back and settle the score himself, government marshal be damned." He was not grinning now. His face was hard and sober. "You believe that much, don't you?"

"If I did, what difference would it make? I've got no business with you, Somerson."

"Just a minute; you haven't heard it all yet. Remember, this is the truth — your pa's in trouble, kid. The rebel army we rode for in Mexico got whipped; the ringleaders are bein' shot where they find 'em. That's why I came north. But your pa's not so lucky; he's got no place to run."

Jeff felt an icy finger move up his spine. "How do I know this ain't another lie?"

"You don't," Somerson said bluntly. "You could find out if you wanted to write the authorities on the Border. But you won't. Because you can see I'm tellin' the truth, can't you?"

Jeff tried to tell himself differently, but he instinctively knew that this was the truth, just as the other had been a lie. His legs felt suddenly weak. "Let's hear the rest of it," he said quietly.

"It's the simplest thing in the world. Your Pa needs money. It wouldn't help him much in Texas, but in Mexico he can buy himself onto the right side of the law." Now he grinned again, but this time the expression did not reach as far as his eyes. "With plenty of luck, I'd say your pa has about a month to go before they catch him. Do you know how they execute rebels in Mexico, kid? First, they make you dig your own grave, then they tie your hands and feet and bring in the firing squad. Mexicans are lousy shots, especially the ones they put in firing squads. They shoot you in the gut, if they can, and while you're still yellin' they start shovelin' dirt in —"

"That's enough!" Jeff snarled.

"Makes you squeamish, doesn't it? But that's the way they do it. That's the way it'll happen to Nate, if he doesn't get help. Five thousand dollars, kid. Is it worth that much to save your pa from a Mexican firing squad?"

Jeff felt his insides shrinking. He didn't even have enough to pay for his sleeping room.

Somerson saw that he was winning, and pushed hard. "Plainsville's a lively town these days," he said. "Farmers bringin' their crops in, a lot of cattle money changin' hands. There's plenty of cash in that bank for a man smart enough to get it — enough to save your pa, kid, and then some."

Jeff could not think. His brain felt as cold and immovable as stone. "What could I do?" he asked numbly. "Why did you pick me?"

"That's easy, kid." Somerson picked up the coffee can, poured in a little cool water from his canteen to settle the grounds, then drank from the tin lip. "First, you're Nate Blaine's boy, so I figure you've got the guts for this kind of thing. Next, I'm not afraid you'll do any dangerous talkin'. Finally, and most important, you know the town and everybody there knows you. That's goin' to be important, as you'll see later."

"What about your friend Fay. Why don't you get him to help you?"

"He will. Here, you'd better have some of this coffee, kid. You look like your nerves could use it."

It was almost noon when Jeff headed back toward Plainsville. Somerson walked across the weed-grown yard with him to get the claybank. "It has to be on the first of the month," the outlaw was saying. "Everybody does his bankin' around then, so there should be plenty of cash in the vault. How do you feel?"

"How am I supposed to feel?" Jeff asked bitterly.

Somerson's voice was suddenly a snarl. "You listen to me, kid, and listen good! If you want your pa dead, you just go back to town and forget all about this. But if you want to save Nate's neck, you do as I say!"

When Jeff said nothing, the outlaw grabbed his arm. "You write the Border rangers, if you don't believe what I'm tellin' you about Nate!"

"Get your hand off me."

Somerson blinked in surprise, then dropped his hand. He could almost believe that Nate himself had spoken. "Sure, kid, I didn't mean to grab. Well, you go back to town and think over what I told you. I'll have Milan Fay contact you when the time is right."

Jeff swung stiffly to the saddle and said nothing.

CHAPTER SIXTEEN

Jeff left the claybank in the alley behind Ludlow's store. It had been twenty-four hours since he had slept, his nerves were jumpy, and there was sickness in the pit of his stomach. Through the long ride back he had pondered Somerson's proposition and still had no answer.

Now it was night again, Sunday night and gravely quiet. No pianos, no fiddles, no dancing. Main Street was almost deserted; the cowhands had slept off their drunks, and the dancers had gone home. He could hear the whispered rattle of the wheel of fortune in Bert Surratt's place, and that seemed to be the only sound in the whole town.

Wearily, Jeff loosened the cinch on the claybank, unbitted the animal and tied it to graze behind the store. Where Milan Fay was, he did not know.

He tramped heavily toward the outside stairs that led to the rooms above Ludlow's store. He climbed the stairway and stood for a moment on the landing, looking down at the sleeping town. This, he thought, is where my pa was raised, and where I was born. It's the only place I know.

The thought hung, suspended in his mind. How would it feel to cut yourself away from the only world you knew? Nathan had done it. Somerson was going to do it, and Milan Fay. How did they get along, those men?

Then he thought angrily that all he needed was some sleep. He'd be damned if he'd get sentimental about a town that had done its best to break him.

His spurs rang softly as he walked down the hot hallway; the boards squeaked under the thud of his boot heels. His door was partly open. He shoved it open the rest of the way and saw the tall, lean-faced man lying across his bunk.

"What are you doing here?" he said to Milan Fay.

Obviously Fay had been asleep, but he came awake instantly, flipping over the edge of the bed with the quickness of a cat. In the white starlight, Jeff could see the revolver pointed at his middle. Fay had been sleeping with it in his hand.

He recognized Jeff and said, "That's a dangerous thing to do, comin' on a man sudden that way!"

"What are you doing in my room?"

"Can you think of a better place to wait?" Fay said calmly, dropping his Colt's into its holster. "I don't think people know me in this town, but there's no sense takin' chances." He kept his voice quiet, for the sound of snoring drifted through the thin walls like the drone of bees.

"How long have you been a friend of Somerson's?" Jeff asked curiously.

The man laughed softly. "Didn't he tell you?" Then he sat on the edge of the bed, flipped makings from his shirt pocket and skillfully built a brown-paper cigarette, Mexican style. He looked at Jeff and shrugged, as though he had been by himself for a long time and wanted to talk to someone.

"I've known Somerson off and on for a good spell," he said easily. "He's a lousy gambler and too fast to get his bile up, but he's as good as the next to team with. I warned him he'd get in trouble usin' a holdout in a town like this."

"You were here when he shot Costain?" Jeff asked, surprised.

Fay laughed silently. "Sure, but not in Surratt's place. That holdout contraption he had up his sleeve; I told him he'd never get away with it."

It was a brilliant night, white with the light from moon and stars. Jeff could see the touch of dry amusement on the man's face. Somerson's getting caught at cheating and Costain's getting shot was all a kind of bitter joke to him. Fay held a match to his cigarette and said, "What did you and Somerson decide on, kid?"

"Why did you and Somerson come to Plainsville?" Jeff asked, as though he hadn't heard the question.

"What did Somerson tell you?"

"That my pa was in trouble and had to have money to square himself with the Mexican authorities."

Fay looked faintly surprised. "It's the truth," he nodded. "You can check it with the Border rangers, if you want to. I'm kind of surprised that Somerson told you, though. He's against the truth, as a matter of principle."

"How much do you know about Somerson's plans?"

"First," Fay said softly, "you tell me what kind of a deal you two struck up. Are you throwin' with us?"

Jeff turned to the single dirty window and stared again at the town. "I don't know," he said at last. "I'll have to think about it."

Fay smoked his cigarette in silence. Then he got up. "Sure," he said, starting for the door, and this time there was no amusement in his voice. It was flat and deadly. "You think about it, kid. In the meantime Nate may be dyin'."

The door opened and closed, and Fay's big rowels made silver music in the dark hallway. Jeff stood rigidly at the window. Suddenly he turned, his fists clenched. He knew that Fay and Somerson had him. They could make him do anything they pleased. He had no choice.

The next morning he awoke to find the huge, bulldog figure of Elec Blasingame standing in the doorway. Jeff sat up in his underwear, reaching for his pants. "I'm going to have to see Frank Ludlow about puttin' a lock on my door."

"You took a trip yesterday," the marshal said bluntly. "Where?"

The aggressiveness in the marshal's tone set fire to Jeff's anger. "I figure that's none of your business, Elec," he said shortly.

"And you had a caller last night, too. Who was it?"

Jeff blinked in surprise, but soon recovered. "I figure that's none of your business, either."

"You listen to me," Blasingame said, and obviously he was angry. He came into the room and slammed the door. "I don't talk just to hear my head rattle; I want answers. Was it your pa you went to see last night when I let you out of jail? Is Nate hidin' out in this part of Texas?"

This time Jeff was truly surprised. He forgot his anger for a moment and gazed at the marshal with blank curiosity. "What makes you ask that? You know Nathan's in Mexico."

"Is he?" Elec flashed a yellow paper in Jeff's face. "This is a telegram from the marshal at Fort Smith. They say Nate's up to his neck in Mexican trouble, and may try to get back across the Border. He's wanted for killin' in New Mexico, and I'll get him, son. If he comes back to Plainsville, I'll get him."

Something inside Jeff's chest went hard. So Somerson and Fay had been telling the truth. It was no surprise, for men like them were as brazen with truth as with lies. But coming from Elec Blasingame it sounded more real and deadly.

Jeff pulled on his pants, then buttoned his shirt to keep his hands busy. Not looking at the marshal, he said, "I didn't see Nathan last night, if that's what you're wondering."

"Then who?"

Jeff clamped his jaws and buckled on his gun.

"Where'd you get that claybank that you rode last night?"

Didn't he ever sleep? Jeff wondered. Did he see everything that happened in this town?

"How long have you known Milan Fay?" Elec went on doggedly.

Jeff felt a hard band tighten around his heart. He glanced quickly at Elec, then began pulling on his boots. "I never heard of Milan Fay."

"He's the man who was in your room last night when you got back from your ride," the marshal said dryly. "He's the man who owns the claybank. Now what do you know about him?"

Jeff kept his grim silence.

"Is he a friend of your pa's? He looks the type. He's been south, too, from the look of his spurs." Elec strode angrily to the bed and made Jeff look at him. "If Fay and Nate have teamed up, I'll find out about it."

"That's your job," Jeff said bitterly. "If you want to make a fool of yourself, I won't try to stop you."

"Then what have you got to do with Milan Fay, if he's not tied up with Nate? The man's a hardcase, maybe a killer. I knew it the minute I saw him get off the train."

Blasingame frowned, his small eyes brilliant with concentration. "By hell, Fay got off with that gambler that shot Phil Costain! I hadn't thought of that!" Thoughtfully, Elec rubbed his chin with the back of his hand. "The gambler, and Fay, and the son of Nate Blaine," he chanted quietly, almost to himself. "Now that may be something to think about."

Jeff laughed, but the sound rang false and unconvincing.

The marshal looked at him for a long moment. "We'll see," he said, turning abruptly and tramping out of the room.

For a long while Jeff sat unmoving, his mind racing. He knew that he'd go through with the robbery, for Nathan's sake. But he didn't like the way Elec was tying things together.

Walk gently, he told himself. He was a long way from shore and the ice was thin. He could almost hear it cracking . . .

Outside, the sun was already blasting away at the prairie, and the airless room became uninhabitable. For a moment, before leaving, Jeff Blaine regarded this room of his, this home that he had made for himself. The sagging bunk with its straw mattress, the scaling bureau, the crockery pitcher and bowl and the oil lamp. Once, not long ago, he had owned two sections of land and had had money in his pocket. Now he had nothing. Not even enough to pay the rent on this room at the end of the week.

Then he remembered that it wouldn't matter about the rent. The first of the month was only three days off — and then he'd put Plainsville behind him, for good.

Strangely, the thought did not please him. He had clung to this place because it was the only one he had. He told himself that he'd be better off for leaving the town, but agreement did not come easily. At last he pulled his hat on and strode angrily out of the room.

He had only one possession which he could trade for money. He pawned his Colt's with Sam Baxter for twelve dollars and came out of the store feeling strangely naked and ashamed. He told himself that it was a temporary thing, that he could pick up enough money at seven-up or twenty-one to reclaim the gun.

In the eating house, he took a booth in the back. As he was cutting into his eggs and side meat, Jeff saw Milan Fay's tall figure in the doorway. The man raked the house with his dark eyes, spotted Jeff quickly, and headed toward the booth.

Jeff looked up angrily. "Are you crazy, coming in here like this?"

Fay folded his lanky frame into the booth. "What's the matter, kid? You look jumpy."

"I've got a right to look jumpy," Jeff said tightly. "Elec Blasingame paid me a visit this morning. He's beginning to tie us together — me, you, and Somerson."

Fay's eyes narrowed. "How does he figure that?"

"He saw you get off the train with Somerson. And he knows I borrowed your claybank."

Unexpectedly, the tall man laughed. "He's just throwin' out some wild guesses. I'll get out of town and stay clear, if that'll make you feel easier. But I've got to take word back to Somerson about the bank job. What do you say, Blaine?"

"I'm ready. I've got no choice."

Milan Fay allowed himself a small smile. "Somerson will be glad to hear it. So will your pa. Did Somerson tell you exactly what he wanted you to do?"

"Yes."

"Then that settles it, I guess." Fay worked himself out of the booth. "We'll be seein' you, kid."

Jeff sat for a moment after Fay had disappeared on the street, his appetite gone. He wondered how a person went about the business of forgetting. How many days and nights would the vision of Amy Wintworth cling to his mind before he finally caught on to this business of forgetting her?

Far to the south that night a gaunt, big-boned man rode by starlight, hugging the high ground. He traveled as the cavalry travels in forced march, now riding, now leading, now resting. His big head thrown back with a savage pride, he kept his face to the north. He avoided the valleys and the lowlands scrupulously, keeping always to the ridges and crests of the prairie, his dark eyes intense and watchful.

He did not build fires. Once every twelve hours he would pause for a while to chew on tasteless jerked beef. He would feed his animal a few handfuls of corn that he carried in a sack behind the saddle, and he would unsaddle and unbit and let the horse graze in the scant grass of the hills. His own comfort and well-being seemed not to concern him, but with the horse he was attentive and gentle.

They had come a long way together, the man and the animal; they had as far yet to travel, and the time was short. The man knew his own weariness by the ache of his bones, by the cotton in his mouth and by the sourness of his stomach. He could scratch at the crust of filth which covered him as a second skin and feel the crawling of ticks from the brush and lice from the desert.

He did not wash, for water was rare in the hills and must be saved for the animal. The saddle sores on the animal's back must be attended to, lice must be brushed from flanks and chest and legs, and hoofs must be cared for and kept clean.

The man had no time for himself. He must move always to the north and the horse must carry him. With mounting impatience, he paced the rocky ground while the animal grazed, he grabbed snatches of sleep at odd moments, and he kept his Colt's and Winchester clean. Soon he would be off again.

CHAPTER SEVENTEEN

Wirt Sewell awoke to heavy, monotonous pounding. He lay in groggy drowsiness, listening. Beulah stirred restlessly beside him.

"It's the door," Beulah said peevishly. "Wirt, what time is it?"

"I don't know. Too dark to see my watch."

"Well, get up and light the lamp, and see who's pounding on our door this time of night."

Wirt climbed out of bed. "All right!" he said thickly, and the monotonous pounding continued while he fumbled for a match and got the lamp wick burning evenly. In his long cotton nightshirt he made his way stiffly into the parlor and opened the door.

He didn't recognize the face at first. It was stiff and ugly with a filth-matted beard, the thin lips cracked and gray with dust. But the eyes were the same.

"Wirt," Beulah called from the bedroom, "who it is?"

Wirt's dread was like a nightmare come to life. He felt himself shrink inside until his heart was a small, cold knot. In the back of his mind he could still hear Elec Blasingame saying: *some day Nate Blaine will come back to Plainsville. When he does, I wouldn't want to be in your place, or your wife's.*

"You look surprised, Wirt," Nathan said coldly, pushing his way into the room.

Clutching the lighted lamp in both hands, Wirt began backing away, his eyes wide.

"Wirt!" Beulah called impatiently. "Tell me who it is!"

Nathan hooked the front door with a spur and slammed it. Without raising his voice he said, "It's your brother-in-law, Beulah — the one you saw kill Jed Harper."

To Wirt, the voice was as cold and deadly as the .45 on Nathan's thigh. He tried to speak, but the words stuck in his throat and were cracked and warped when they finally came out. "Nate, for God's sake, what are you going to do!"

"Why, nothing, Wirt. Not just yet, anyway."

Now Wirt realized that Nathan's voice was flat and emotionless, and that all the hate was in his eyes. Although he had made no show of violence, Wirt knew that violence was in the room, ready to explode.

When Beulah appeared in the doorway, clutching a white wrapper that covered her frail body from her chin to the floor, Nathan merely inclined his head in a hint of a nod. "Hello, Beulah. How have you been sleeping these past five years?"

Beulah Sewell's face was whiter than the wrapper. The old aggressive thrust of her small chin was missing now, and her eyes were strangely vacant.

Nathan laughed suddenly, harshly. "I guess you haven't been sleeping so well, at that. I never would have thought you'd be bothered by your conscience, Beulah."

He came deeper into the room and dropped slowly into a parlor chair. He sighed softly, stretching his long legs in front of him. Wirt felt that he could almost see eddies of fatigue swirling around Nathan's lean, tough figure, like heat eddies rising over a desert. Until now Beulah had not made a sound, but now she moved slowly into the room, her eyes as blank as a sleepwalker's.

"Why did you come back?" she asked softly.

"Didn't you think I would?" His voice was toneless.

Wirt shot his wife a quick glance of warning, but she didn't see it. Nathan sat like a dead man, his arms hanging limp at his sides. Only his eyes were alive as he stared at Beulah.

"I came back to see my boy," he said at last.

"Haven't you done enough to him?" Beulah asked flatly, ignoring her husband's look of panic. "Aren't you satisfied?"

Hard lines of anger appeared for the first time at the corners of Nathan's mouth. "Haven't I done enough to him! How about you, Beulah? What have you done to him?" With an unexpected burst of energy, he shoved himself out of the chair. "Haven't I done enough to him!" he demanded again, angrily.

As suddenly as the outburst was born, it died. He dropped back to the chair and said wearily, "Heat some wash water for me, Beulah. And I could do with some coffee, too, and some grub."

Beulah acted as though she hadn't heard. Her husband said quickly, "Do as he says, Beulah!"

Reluctantly, she turned for the kitchen.

After a moment Nathan turned to Wirt. "Where's the boy?"

"He's still here, Nate. Here in Plainsville."

"I know that; where's he staying?"

"In a room over Frank Ludlow's store, I think."

"Go rout him out and tell him his pa's come home."

"Now, Nate?" Wirt said uneasily. "This time of night?"

"Right now! And don't let Elec Blasingame see you, either. Or anybody else."

Wirt swallowed. "I'll be careful, Nate."

"You'd better! And if you've got any ideas about turnin' me in to the law, you better think about it a long time. Remember, I'll be waitin' here with Beulah, and I haven't got much cause to like her."

Wirt's voice cracked. "Nate, you know I wouldn't do a thing like that."

Nathan looked at him, then he closed his eyes and rested his head back against the chair. "Get going," he said quietly, and Wirt stumbled over his own feet on the way for his clothes.

Jeff was in his bunk, but not asleep; he heard the loose boards creek as Wirt made his way up the outside stairs. He lay for a moment, tensely alert, as the footsteps came nearer. There was a timid rap at the door.

Jeff reached for his revolver. "Who is it?"

"It's Wirt. I've got to talk to you, Jeff!"

"Get away from me!"

"Jeff, it's important!"

Jeff lay on one elbow, listening to his own breathing. What could be important enough to bring Wirt Sewell here at this time of night? At last he got up and slipped the inside latch. "What do you want?"

"Jeff, your pa's back. He's at the house right now!"

For several seconds Jeff did not move. Nathan was back! Didn't he know that the law was looking for him?

His calmness surprised him. "Wait," he said, then he got into his pants and shirt, and pulled on his boots. Buckling his cartridge belt, he turned back to Wirt. "How is he? Is he all right?"

"I — I guess so."

"You guess so? Don't you know? He's not hurt, is he?"

"No, Jeff, he's not hurt. Not in body."

Jeff gave him a hard, savage look, but said nothing. Why had Nathan come back?

He said, "We'll go out the back way. Follow me."

At the far end of the hall there was a window, with a plank ladder outside that served as a fire escape. It was late, and the town was quiet. Jeff stepped through the open window, grabbed the ladder and swung out. When he reached the ground he didn't look back to see if Wirt had made it — he didn't care.

The pounding of his heart was the only sound he heard as he slipped behind the building and up the alley. At the end of Main Street he cut across town, heading toward the Sewell house, vaguely aware of Wirt stumbling behind.

The Sewell house was the only place in that part of town that still had a light burning. Jeff came in behind the cowshed, noted the trail-shaggy calico standing hipshot and weary beside the Sewell cow. When he reached the back door he went through without knocking.

Nathan had just finished washing and shaving. His face looked sunken, raw and red, and he stood motionless for a moment, a towel over his shoulder, looking steadily at his son. Then, with that old gesture that Jeff remembered so well, he threw back his head and searched Jeff's face. And he was the same Nathan Blaine that Jeff remembered, big and proud and dark with danger.

"You're a man," Nathan said at last. "I don't think I'd figured on that."

"Almost nineteen," Jeff said evenly.

"Plenty old enough for a man in these parts."

"Pa," Jeff said, suddenly uncomfortable, "you're all right, aren't you? I mean —"

"I'm fine! A little trail dirty, maybe, but fine."

And then, as though a wall between them had been scaled, Nathan came forward and took his son's hand, and all the fierce love that was in them expressed itself in that one hard clasp.

They heard Wirt stumbling across the back yard, and suddenly both men, father and son, let go and made an elaborate show of being casual. Nathan turned to the table, where greens and cornbread had been set out by Beulah. "I hear the government boys are looking for me," he said mildly, beginning to eat.

"They've contacted the marshal here," Jeff said. "Now he's looking for you, too."

"Elec Blasingame? He couldn't find his nose with both hands."

Both of them laughed, but it had a false ring. Nathan's danger increased with every minute he stayed here, and Jeff knew it.

They looked hard at Wirt as he came in the back door, and said nothing more until he had passed through to the parlor. Jeff said, "I guess you heard what happened?"

"About them finding the man that killed Jed Harper? Yes, I heard." His voice was mild enough, but Jeff noticed that Nathan kept his eyes on the plate before him and did not look up. "How did the town take it?"

"I guess Beulah Sewell will never be able to look the people of this town in the eye again," Jeff answered with sudden bitterness.

Now Nathan did look up, faintly surprised. "Is that so? And what did you do, Jeff, when you found out?"

"I did what anybody would have done. I got out of the Sewell house! I never wanted to see them again."

A fine network of lines appeared around Nathan's eyes. "You hate them, don't you?"

"Sure I hate them! Don't you?"

The question seemed to surprise Nathan. He put his fork down slowly and seemed to study the question in all its aspects, and only then did he answer. "Yes. I hate them." Abruptly, he stood up and shouted, "Beulah, bring some coffee to the parlor!"

With cool authority, Nathan ordered Wirt and his wife to another part of the house when he and Jeff came to the parlor. Not until then did Jeff see how much older his father looked, how tired his eyes were, how deep in his face were the lines of anger. "Yes," Nate said again, sinking heavily into a chair, "I hate them. There's no sense denying it."

"Why should you, after what Beulah did?"

Nathan smiled thinly, almost to himself. "Hate, as you'll learn, gets to be a heavy load when you can't put it down." Then he asked bluntly, "How well do you know Bill Somerson?"

Jeff blinked in surprise. How could Nathan know about Somerson?

Again Nathan smiled his thin smile. "Among Indians and outlaws, word has a way of traveling fast. What you and Somerson are cooking together, I don't know, but I know it's something."

Jeff felt the breath of warning in Nathan's smile. "I turned a posse off Somerson's trail once," he said carefully. "That's about all I know about him."

Surprisingly, his father let it drop. He sat in silence for a moment, his eyes closed. Then he said, "I know how you feel about this town, but there's something I want to know. Is there anything about it that you like and would hate to leave?"

As though a door in his mind had been opened, the vision of Amy was suddenly there. Too late did Jeff realize that Nathan's eyes were not completely closed and that he was watching his face intently from under his black lashes. And then Nathan did close his eyes, and for a moment the deep lines around his mouth did not seem so harsh.

"I remember," he said, "when I wasn't much older than you are now and I had a reason for staying in Plainsville. But when your mother died —" Then he discarded the thought as suddenly as he had dropped Somerson.

Jeff shook his head, bewildered. "Why did you take the chance of coming back here? Was it because of me?"

Nathan only looked at him.

"Are things so bad in Mexico that you couldn't stay there?"

His father seemed surprised. "You know about that?"

"Everybody does, I guess. Elec Blasingame does; that's why he expects you to head back for Texas."

Unexpectedly, Nathan laughed. "Nothing ever gets so bad in Mexico that you can't put it right with money."

"And you have the money?"

"Of course."

But Jeff could see that it was a brazen lie. That stunted calico in the cowshed, the clothes that Nathan wore — those things did not suggest money. And perhaps Nathan could see what was in his son's mind, for the worry lines around his eyes seemed to deepen.

"Don't you start worrying about your pa," he said sternly. "Nathan Blaine can take care of himself. It's you I'm worried about."

"Why should you worry about me?"

For a moment he thought he would get no answer. Nathan shoved himself forward in his chair and studied his lean, strong hands. "Will you make me a promise?" he finally asked. "Don't act the fool, the way I did at your age, and get yourself into trouble that you can't get out of. Don't listen to stories about Nate Blaine being in bad with the Mexicans, either." He laughed shortly, but not with his eyes. "I can't imagine how that story got started. Why, I'm heading back for the Border tomorrow, as soon as my horse gets rested up. Would I be doing a thing like that if there was trouble?"

Jeff cleared his throat, but said nothing.

"What I'm trying to say," Nathan continued, "is that I don't need your help. Nate Blaine needs help from nobody. Is that clear?"

Jeff nodded.

"If you hate this town, that's all right with me. But think it over before you kick it for the last time and put it behind you."

Puzzled, Jeff didn't know what the talk was getting around to.

"All I want is your promise," Nathan said.

"You oughtn't worry about me," Jeff said evasively. "You said yourself I was a man."

"But I still want the promise that you're not headed for trouble on my account. I rode a long way just to hear it."

Jeff thought, When it comes to lying, I can do it just as brazenly as he can. "Sure," he said, "I promise." He did not realize how tense Nathan had been until he watched him now slowly relaxing, unwinding painfully, like a taut steel spring.

"Good," Nathan said. "Now you'd better go back to your room — we can't attract attention by keeping these lights on."

"When will I see you again?"

"I don't know. Maybe you'll come to Mexico some time and look me up."

"You're leaving so soon?"

His anxiety was all too obvious in his voice, and Nathan smiled faintly. "Don't look as though you'll never see me again. It's just Mexico — not so far."

Nathan had said it, and the dead coldness in the pit of his stomach told Jeff that it was true. If his pa went back to Mexico without the money to pay for his life, he would never see him again. They shook hands silently.

At the door, Nathan said, "There's just one more thing . . ." Jeff thought that Nathan had forgotten it, but what he said, "Somerson's bad medicine. Have nothing to do with him."

CHAPTER EIGHTEEN

It was the first of the month. Milan Fay was on time.

"Somerson's got everything set, kid. You ready?"

"Yes."

"You know how it's going? Exactly?"

"Yes."

Fay shook his head in faint surprise. "Damn if you don't look ready, at that. I guess you're Nate Blaine's boy, all right."

"Don't worry. I'll be in place at four o'clock."

The tall outlaw grinned. "That's the kind of talk I like to hear. But don't make a move until I get the wagon in place."

"I know my part of it," Jeff said shortly. "Just make sure you and the horses are where they're supposed to be."

"It's not me or Somerson or the horses that I'll be thinkin' about, kid; you're the one. Just remember your pa's life depends on whether or not we bring this off without a hitch."

Jeff watched Fay's broad, arrogant back as he turned and sauntered up the plank walk toward the public corral. No one had to tell him to be careful, or how dangerous this thing was going to be. Plainsville was no longer a one-horse cowtown. It was a railroad town and farm town as well, and the bank was no longer the flimsy unprotected affair that it had once been.

But it was set. There was no backing out. And he wouldn't have done it if he could . . .

In his basement office of the Masonic Temple, Elec Blasingame heard the click of heels on the stone steps and knew that they were not boot heels. Breathlessly, Amy Wintworth came into the room, and the marshal looked up in surprise.

"What's the matter, child? You look as if somebody's chasing you."

"Marshal, I've got to talk to you! Alone."

Kirk Logan, who was nailing a calendar to the far wall of the office, looked around at the last word. The marshal frowned slightly, but then nodded to his deputy, and Logan put his hammer down and walked out. During those few seconds Elec made a close study of the girl before him. He noted her tenseness, the look of urgency in her eyes.

"Now," he said, "what is it, Amy?"

"Nathan Blaine is in Plainsville."

Blasingame was startled. "Nate Blaine! How do you know?"

"I saw him. I talked to him."

"Here in Plainsville?" His voice was incredulous. But before Amy could answer one question he asked another. "Where's he hiding?"

"He was at the Sewell house —" Amy started, and the marshal lunged up from his desk and bellowed, "Kirk, get in here on the run!"

But there was something about the quick, hard look that the girl threw at him that made him look at her again. "Marshal," she said tightly, "you don't understand. Nathan Blaine isn't hiding. He asked me to come here and tell you he wants to see you."

Elec didn't believe it. "Nate Blaine wants to see me?"

"Please believe me!" she said anxiously. "He wants to talk to you about Jeff."

Then a frowning Kirk Logan came back in the office. "What's the trouble, Marshal?" For a moment Elec was undecided. It didn't make sense that Nate Blaine would walk into a sure arrest — an arrest that could possibly end with a hangman's noose around his neck. Still, there was something about the urgency in Amy's face that made him pause. At last, against his better judgment, he waved the puzzled deputy away again.

"If Nate's here in Plainsville," he said, "I guess a few minutes one way or the other won't make too much difference. Now, Amy, start at the beginning and tell me all you know."

Amy looked nervously at her hands, wondering how she could explain it to the marshal when she was unable to explain it to herself. "I was shopping this morning," she began slowly. "I was in Baxter's when Mr. Sewell found me and said Jeff's father was at their house and wanted to see me."

Elec scowled. "Why did he want to see you?"

"I'm not sure."

"But you did talk to Nate? What about?"

He realized too late that this was no cowhand that he could shout at and bully into telling him what he wanted to know. He saw the spark of resentment in those clear eyes, and the haughty tilt of her chin.

"I'm sorry, Amy," he said lamely. "Tell it your own way."

She didn't know how or where to start. She could still feel the shock of Nathan's fierce gaze upon her. The depression that came from staring too deeply into the bitterness of those dark eyes was still within her.

"So you're the girl my boy loves," he had said, and the gentleness of his voice had startled her. She had hated Nathan Blaine for so long, and she could not believe that such contradictions as gentleness and violence could live together within one body.

But when Nathan Blaine had spoken of his son, he was gentle. And then he had asked with crude bluntness: "Do you love my boy, Amy?" She had never been talked to like that before. She had tried to wither him with her anger, but he stood like a statue hacked from steel.

"Do you love him?" he had asked again, coldly. His question demanded the truth, and left no way for a middle ground of indecision. Wirt and Beulah had stood looking on, frightened.

She had answered, "Yes."

"I don't believe it!" he replied brutally. "When Jeff needed you most, you deserted him. When he wanted understanding, you wrapped yourself in pride."

Deep within her conscience she knew he was right, and it had made her furious. "And what about you?" she'd flared. "You, his own father — what have you done for him?"

In dismay she had watched the power seep out of him as he smiled thinly and sank into one of the uncomfortable parlor chairs. "Yes," he had said, almost absently. "I guess I ought to stop blaming others and do something myself. Do you know where Elec Blasingame's office is? Would you tell the marshal I'd like to see him? In private."

She had stood woodenly, with pity in her eyes. Nathan had seen it and was furious. "What are you waitin' on?" he had demanded harshly. "I thought you'd jump at the chance to turn me in!"

Wirt had started to go with her, but Nathan had barked, "Stay here, Wirt." Then, to Amy: "Remember, tell the marshal I want to see him in private. If you tell anybody else, or if he brings a posse with him —" He had smiled. "Remember I've got Wirt and Beulah right here with me."

Amy had run blindly from the house, both hate and pity churning within her. Not until she had reached the marshal's office did she fully realize that Nathan had planned it so. He was used to being hated, feared — but Nathan Blaine was not the kind of man to accept pity.

So she tried to tell Elec Blasingame what had happened, but there was no way she could communicate to another what she had seen and felt instinctively. She ended lamely, "I think Jeff's in trouble, and that's what Nathan wants to talk to you about."

"That boy's been getting deeper in trouble for a long time," Elec scowled. "I think this is a trick of Nate's."

But he wasn't sure. And if he had been sure, there was very little he could do about it, with Wirt and Beulah Sewell being held as hostages.

He would have to play it Nate's way, whether he liked it or not. "All right," he said finally. "I'll go. But you stay here, Amy, until I get back." Before heading for the stairs, he called to Kirk Logan. "Get on the street, Kirk, and see if you can find young Blaine. Keep your eye on him, but don't let him see you watching him. Understand?"

The deputy nodded, puzzled. "Sure, but why?"

"Never mind; just do as I say." Then, halfway up the steps, Elec thought of something else. He wasn't sure that it meant anything, but this was no time to take chances. "By the way, Kirk, that gambler in town that goes under the name of Milan Fay — the one that hangs out at the Green House. Keep an eye on him too, if you can. Let me know what they're doing — I'll be at the Sewell place."

It was a quiet day for Plainsville. The homesteaders were out working the land; the cattle shipping was about over till the next season. A merciless sun blazed down on the town and on Elec Blasingame as he tramped up the plank walk to the bank corner, then cut across town toward the Sewell place. The marshal had no choice in the matter. Nate was calling the tune this time, and Elec had to dance to it.

But that didn't mean that Elec was helpless, trick or no trick. As he went up the path to the Sewell house he loosened his revolver in its holster. His duty was to arrest Nate Blaine, and he was going to do it if he could.

The front door stood open because of the heat, but the front parlor was as dark as a cave to the marshal's sun-blinded eyes. Now he unholstered his .45 and held it at his side as he stepped up to the front porch. Suddenly the doorway was filled with Nate Blaine's big figure, and Elec immediately snapped his gunhand to the ready and said, "Don't move, Nate! You're under arrest."

Now, if it was a trick, he would soon know it.

Nathan glared at him for a moment, angrily. "I'm not armed, Elec. You can put your gun away."

But Elec made no move to holster the gun. He hooked the screen door with the toe of his boot and kicked it open. "Back in the room, Nate," he said sharply, "and don't try anything."

He came to Nathan like a bull, shoving him back in the room with the muzzle of his .45. From the corner of his eye he saw Wirt and Beulah standing pale and frightened against the far wall. He saw Nate's revolver hanging harmlessly on the hatrack in the hall. Quickly but methodically, the marshal added up every fact within the range of his senses.

It didn't seem like a trick, which made him believe all the more that it was one. "Wirt," he said, without shifting his gaze from Nathan, "what's he up to? Are you and your wife all right?"

Wirt swallowed hard. "We're all right, Marshal. He had me find the Wintworth girl for him, then he sent her to bring you. That's all I know."

Nathan said angrily, "I wanted to talk to you. Can't you understand a simple thing like that?"

"No, I can't," Blasingame said harshly. "You know you're wanted in Texas, as well as some other places. You knew I'd put you under arrest. I've never seen the man who'd deliberately ask for twenty years in prison, or maybe even a hangman's noose."

With fire and danger swimming in those black eyes, Nathan snarled, "Stop being a fat fool, Elec, and put that gun away! If I'd wanted to kill you I'd have shot you from the window as you came up the walk. I'm not an idiot; I know I'm under arrest. But I'll be arrested under my own conditions, Marshal Blasingame, and don't you forget it!"

It had been a long, long time since any man had talked that way to Elec Blasingame. He was more startled than angered. And then, surprisingly, he found himself reholstering his Colt's. In some way it was impossible to explain he knew that this was no trick, no trap. After a long, careful moment of thought, he said, "All right, Nate, what's on your mind?"

"It's the boy," Nathan said bluntly.

"What about the boy?"

Nathan rubbed a hand over one lean, hard cheek. "I'm not sure. I don't think he's in any big trouble yet, but he's headed there. News like that travels fast in the out-country. Do you know a hardcase by the name of Bill Somerson, heavy-set, red face?"

Elec's eyes narrowed. "What about him?"

"He rode with my outfit in Mexico till they sent him packing. He knows what happened to me up here, about the bank — all of it. I told him, under a load of wine, and it gave him ideas. The story I heard from the other side of the Border was that Somerson was fixing up something with my boy."

"And you came all the way from Mexico to stop it?" Elec asked.

"Wouldn't you, if he was your boy?"

The marshal let that pass. "I don't believe you, Nate," he said flatly. "The boy's been heading for trouble ever since you went to work on him five years ago."

"Damn it!" Nathan exploded, his powerful shoulders twitching. "He's heading for trouble on my account; that's the reason I came back! He knows I'm in Mexican trouble and that I need money to get out of it. So he's going after the money."

"By throwin' in with this man called Somerson?"

"How many times do I have to tell you?"

Elec could not miss the note of desperation in Nate Blaine's voice. And in his quick, methodical brain he remembered other things that might tie in with what Nate was telling him. He asked suddenly, "You know a man named Milan Fay?"

Nathan blinked. "Sure. He sided Somerson for a while in Chihuahua."

More facts added up, and Elec felt a vague uneasiness tugging at the ends of his nerves — the ride Jeff had taken on Fay's horse, the fact that Fay and Somerson had arrived in Plainsville on the same train. It could be that the boy was headed for real trouble —

trouble that he'd never get out of. Trouble, Elec thought, like his pa is in now.

He studied Nate quietly for a long while, and once more his memory took him back five years. At that time Nate had all the reason in the world to be full of hate, but he hadn't loaded it on his son. He had kept it bottled within himself and had sent the boy back to Beulah and Wirt.

Maybe, Elec thought carefully, he had underestimated Nathan Blaine's love for his son. And maybe at the same time he had overestimated Nate's selfishness.

Still, that line of reasoning went against the grain with him because he liked things clean-cut, black or white, good or bad. The possibility that a man like Nate might have some good in him as well as bad disturbed the marshal.

Nathan broke in on the marshal's thought. "I came to you for help, Elec. Do I get it?"

The marshal shot quick glances around the room, as though he still expected to uncover a trap. Then he heard the hurried tramp of boots on the clay walk outside the house.

Elec turned on Nathan. "Take it easy, Nate, it's my deputy. He doesn't know you're here." Then he went to the front door where Kirk Logan was waiting.

"What's the trouble, Kirk?"

The deputy shook his head. "Damned if I know, exactly. But I've been keeping my eye on the Blaine kid, like you said, and Milan Fay too. I don't know what kind of trouble you're expectin', Marshal, but it looks like somethin's about to bust. I figured you ought to know."

"I ought to know what?" Elec said impatiently.

"It's just that things look funny. Maybe I wouldn't have noticed anything if you hadn't told me to keep an eye on them, but — Anyway," he shrugged, "I spotted young Blaine talking to Fay in front of Surratt's. They broke up when I went by, but met again in front of Baxter's. After that they walked as far as the bank corner together, then split up again."

"Then what did they do?" Elec asked.

"It's not what they did so much as the way they looked. Blaine went back to Surratt's and got in a seven-up game, but Fay picked him out a fire barrel and sat there like he was starting to keep house, and that's when I began to wonder."

"About what?"

"Just wonder. You said report to you, and I am."

"Where is Fay now?"

"In front of Ludlow's store, just across the street from the bank."

Elec's eyes narrowed. He said, "It's probably nothing, but you'd better get back, anyway. I'll be along pretty soon."

The deputy headed back down the path. As Elec turned, he saw Nathan reaching for his revolver on the hatrack. "Hold it, Nate!" Elec said sharply, his own revolver already in his hand.

"I heard what your deputy said," Nathan said tightly. "This is it, Marshal. It's that bank they're after.

Somerson talked the boy into it; probably told him I had to have the money."

Elec's gun did not waver. "I doubt it. And even if it's true, you're playing no part in it, Nate. You're under arrest, and you're going to jail."

"You're right about just one thing," Nathan said with dangerous calm. "I'm under arrest. I knew that the minute I sent the Wintworth girl after you. But I'm not going to jail until this thing's over — not unless you want to kill me right here."

Elec squeezed the Colt's butt so hard that his arm ached. Nathan ignored it, and he ignored the grim flash of warning in the marshal's eyes.

"If you're going to shoot, you'd better do it now, Elec, before I strap on my gun."

Probably the marshal would never know why he didn't pull the trigger and kill Nate Blaine where he stood. He had not managed to live to an old age by taking chances. Yet, when the time came, he found that he could not make himself add that extra ounce of pressure with his trigger finger. He could not believe that Nate would ignore the certainty of death. He was sure that at the last moment he would back down.

But he did not. Nathan walked steadily, arrogantly even, to the hall hatrack, took down the holster and slung the cartridge belt around his waist. And from the depths of his bitter eyes he poured his quiet disdain upon the marshal.

It was then that Elec realized that he had grown too old for his job. The steel of his resolution had lost its temper, the fine cutting edge of his purpose had dulled.

When he discovered that he could not coldly, calmly pull the trigger on this man who defied him, Elec Blasingame knew he was through as a lawman.

In many ways he was not sorry.

CHAPTER NINETEEN

From his place at Surratt's bar, Jeff saw Amy hurrying across the street toward the Masonic Temple. Impulsively, he went outside, hoping she would notice him, but she didn't look in his direction.

It was just as well he thought. It was nearly four o'clock, and soon his life in Plainsville would be over. Now he was a man called upon to do a man's work. But he felt less a man at that moment than at any time since he had stormed angrily from under the Sewell roof. For the first time in his life he was beginning to know the meaning of fear. It wasn't because of the bank, and what he would have to do there, or the dangerous prospect of violence. This was a different thing.

As he saw Amy disappear down the steps to the marshal's office, he felt his bravery flying with her. His valor, tied to a piece of bright ribbon, went with her down the stone steps and disappeared, and he felt suddenly hollow and afraid.

Angrily, he told himself that he was acting like a boy, and it was time to put boyish things behind him. He knew that Milan Fay had already set the wheels to rolling. By now Fay would have left his place in front of

Ludlow's store to meet Somerson's wagon at the edge of town.

Still, Jeff waited. He saw Elec Blasingame come out of the Masonic Temple basement and head across town to the east. He seemed in a hurry, but he wasn't going toward the bank, and Jeff was glad of that.

He stood for a moment wondering what could bring Elec out in such a hurry, in this heat. Why would Amy be visiting the marshal, and why hadn't she come out when Elec had?

He waited as long as he dared, hoping for another glimpse of Amy, hoping that his bravery would fly back to him.

None of those things happened. He was still a hollow man. But the bank would be robbed, and he would help do it because Nathan's life depended on it. He turned and walked up the plank walk toward the bank.

The timing was perfect.

Fay had already brought the wagon up and was tying the team beside Ludlow's when Jeff reached the corner. It was a heavy farm wagon with a tarp stretched over the sideboards. Under the tarp there might be a load of wheat or corn, but Jeff knew there was nothing at all under it but Bill Somerson, covering the street in both directions with his carbine.

A kind of numbness that passed for calm passed over Jeff, and he was suddenly eager to get it over with. Walking slowly, he noted the horses waiting in the alley behind Ludlow's. He could feel Milan Fay watching from beneath the brim of his shabby hat. Jeff turned the corner and Fay lifted his hand slightly.

Everything was ready.

Jeff forced himself to think of the bank, and put everything else out of his mind. Main Street was normally busy, but the side street was practically deserted. A single buck-board was coming in from the west, and when it turned the corner Fay nodded and Jeff started for the side door of the bank.

Fay sauntered across the street at the same time, walking aimlessly, his quick eyes alert in all directions. Everything was clear. Jeff pounded on the door.

He pounded twice before he got an answer.

"It's Jeff Blaine," he called quietly. "My uncle's Wirt Sewell." Then came a moment of panic and he couldn't think of the new banker's name. Then, as he hesitated, he caught a glimpse of Milan Fay's suspicious scowl, and the name came to him. "Mr. Forney, I'd like to talk to you about some land deeds."

A sharp answer came through the heavy door. "Sorry, the bank's closed for the day. See me at ten tomorrow morning."

Jeff felt sudden sweat on his forehead. This was the reason Somerson had selected him. It was Jeff's job to get in the bank after it had closed, but before the vault had been locked for the night. Attacking the bank during the day with the place full of gun-carrying customers would have been foolish. Waiting until the vault was closed would be hopeless. This was the time it had to be.

Now Jeff could see the deadly purpose in Fay's eyes as the tall man glared at him. He could almost feel the cold steel of Somerson's carbine muzzle, and knew that it was pointed at his back — just in case. "Mr. Forney," he called again, "it's important. There's a good deal of money involved, and it can't wait till tomorrow."

"Who did you say you were?"

"Jefferson Blaine, Wirt Sewell's nephew." Wirt might not be a popular man, but he was known as a good businessman. Then the banker looked out through the barred window beside the door.

"Well, just a minute."

Milan Fay suddenly grinned and moved up beside Jeff, waiting for the door to open. "Good work, kid," he said under his breath. "Nate'll be proud of you for this."

They heard heavy bolts being thrown back and suddenly the door was open. Nathan Blaine stood there with fire in his eyes.

"Hello, Fay," he said coldly.

"Nate!" the tall outlaw said, startled. Jeff could not move. He could not believe that Nathan was actually there. "Nate, what are you doing here?" the tall outlaw asked quickly.

But Milan Fay knew what he was doing there. The fierce fire in Nate Blaine's eyes as he raked his son with a savage glance was enough to tell Fay all he needed to know. Milan Fay was quicker than most to understand such things. And now he understood that Nate knew everything about the way they had tricked the kid into helping them with the bank.

"Where's Somerson?" Nathan demanded coldly.

With the quick instinct of a wolf, Fay understood exactly what he was up against. Nate had learned what he and Somerson were up to and he had come to stop it. As long as Nate stood there, the bank was completely safe. As long as Nate was allowed to bar the way, there would be no robbery.

And Milan Fay had dreamed for a long time about the money they would take from this bank. He and Somerson had made a lot of plans. They had waited patiently for just the right time. And now that the time had come, Fay was determined that no one was going to stop them; not even Nate Blaine.

"Now look here, Nate," Fay started with deceptive mildness. "Of course I don't know what you're thinkin', Nate, but I give you my word —"

It was the oldest trick in the world and the deadliest, talking fast in order to draw attention away from what the gun hand was doing.

But Milan Fay forgot that Nate Blaine had seen all the tricks. The muzzle of Blaine's Colt's had cleared the top of his holster while Fay was still gabbing. Perhaps Fay did not see it. Perhaps he was acting in desperation. He followed through with the snakelike strike of his right hand, and Nathan had no alternative.

The single explosion of Nathan's revolver rocked and bellowed in the empty street, and Milan Fay jackknifed as though some enormous fist had caught him below the heart. The shock of the sound jarred Jeff into action, and in some fragmentary way he realized what Nathan was trying to do for him.

"Look out for Somerson!" he yelled. But Nate only looked at him. The street was empty. Then Elec

Blasingame came pounding heavily around the corner of the bank building.

The ear-splitting crack of Somerson's carbine added its deadly punctuation to the bright afternoon, and the marshal stumbled clumsily, fell against the side of the building, and went to his knees.

Kirk Logan, the deputy, appeared at the other end of the street, but neither Logan nor Nate saw where the shot came from.

"The wagon!" Jeff shouted, but before the words were out, Somerson's carbine spoke again and Nathan went reeling back against the bricks of the building. In a blind rage, Jeff grabbed his Colt's and blasted one, two, three bullets through the sideboards. Nathan was on his knees, shouting something that Jeff could not hear. Anger swept over him like a boiling flood.

Swearing, Nathan got to his feet, then fell again. On his hands and knees he gathered his strength like some maddened bear and threw himself at Jeff's legs. Both of them went crashing down in the dust of the street, and once more Somerson's carbine spoke and the hot slug of lead nailed Nathan to the ground.

Logan was running toward them, but was still too far away to be much help. Then Jeff saw the tarp being ripped back from the wagon's sideboards. He saw Somerson vault with amazing lightness over the side and start running toward the horses.

In one quick second Jeff glanced at Nathan as he lay sprawled in the dust. Only his eyes seemed to live. The gray color of death was already in his face.

In the heart of a hurricane they say there is a great, fantastic calm, where the silence is deafening and all feeling of life and movement is absent. That is the kind of calm that seized Jeff Blaine when he saw Nathan lying at his feet. Slowly, he turned his attention on Somerson's bulky, fleeing figure, and he raised his revolver and aimed carefully, as though it were a target practice and not the deadliest game of all, and he slowly began squeezing the trigger when the sights set steadily in the middle of Somerson's back.

Behind Jeff, Elec Blasingame was pushing himself laboriously to his feet. He was only vaguely aware of the great numbness in his left shoulder and the warm flow of blood down his side. He saw Somerson break out of the wagon and run toward the horses behind Ludlow's store, and he saw Nate Blaine lying as still as death on the ground at his son's feet. Instinctively, the marshal fumbled for his gun, then realized that he had dropped it somewhere when he had taken the carbine slug in his shoulder.

Before he could find his own revolver, Elec saw young Blaine turn his .45 on Somerson's broad, fleeing back. Then something happened that stunned the marshal, for Nathan Blaine was once again lifting himself to his knees, like some mortally wounded animal maddened with pain, pushing, shoving upward. Then, a split second before Jeff's revolver roared, before the heavy bullet ripped its way into Somerson's back, Nathan hurled himself against his son, knocking the boy off balance. The Colt's exploded but the shot went wild, the slug screaming off in the endless sky.

Somerson had reached the horses now. Discarding the carbine, he grabbed his revolver and fired twice across the street. Nate Blaine fell back but stopped himself with an outstretched hand. Then, quickly, as Somerson was climbing hurriedly to the saddle, Nathan fired once, twice, with his own Colt's.

For an instant the impact of the bullets seemed to lift Somerson out of the saddle and hold him there. Then his great hulk fell like stone across the cantle, the frightened horse shied to one side, and Somerson slipped slowly, like poured concrete, to the ground.

Elec put Somerson from his mind. The outlaw would never bother anyone again.

Kirk Logan came running up to Nathan. He glanced quickly at that gray face, those dull eyes, and came on to Elec.

"Are you hurt, Marshal?"

"Nothing I can't get over. But see if you can find Doc Shipley; Nate's going to need some help."

The deputy shook his head. "Nothing Doc Shipley can do, Marshal."

After its moment of flame and violence, the town came under the weight of sudden silence. Then, almost immediately, the marshal heard the pound of boots coming toward them, and the sound of excited voices. Elec turned to Logan and said hoarsely, "Keep the crowd away. Nate has earned the right to die in peace."

The marshal leaned heavily against the building as his deputy headed toward Main Street to hold back the morbid and the curious. He watched the boy kneeling in the dust, holding Nathan's heavy body in his arms. Where numbness had been in Elec's shoulder, now pain burned like a bright flame.

Elec's left arm hung limp and his shirt was plastered to his body with his own blood. Logan led Doc Shipley through, but the marshal pushed him away impatiently. Heavily, he walked into the open street where Nathan lay dead. The marshal was strangely fascinated by the red, wet spots on Nathan's gray face, where the boy's tears had mingled there with the red dust of Plainsville.

Jeff looked up at last and saw the marshal standing there. "Why did he do it?" he asked, his voice hard.

The marshal shifted uncomfortably. "Why did Nate stop you from killing Somerson?" He rubbed the back of his hand over his jowls and tried not to think of the pain in his shoulder. "Maybe it was because Nate knew how bad it is to kill a man, even a man like Somerson. Maybe your pa came to understand that and wanted you to understand it. Maybe it was his way of letting you know that he didn't want you to take the same trail he took so long ago."

After a moment Elec lifted his good arm and motioned for Doc Shipley to take over. He saw Amy Wintworth's white, stunned face in the crowd beside the bank building.

"Marshal, let me talk to him!"

"Not now, Amy."

"But he needs me!"

"Maybe." Elec nodded ponderously. "But what he needs most is to get things straight with himself. Give him time, Amy. Give him time to think."

The next day turned out cool. Great thunderheads had rolled in off the Gulf during the night and a sprinkle of rain had settled the dust. It was a good day for a funeral, Elec Blasingame thought, if any day was a good one for such a thing.

Perhaps the good weather accounted for the big turnout, but Elec doubted it. His left arm bound tightly to his body, the marshal looked over the crowd gathered on the barren slope to the north of town and vaguely wondered what Nathan would think of this if he could see it. Nathan Blaine, a villain in life, was being buried a hero.

Elec regarded this fact wryly but without bitterness. He accepted it as a brutally truthful comment on the conscience of his neighbors. Many of them, he speculated, must have slept uneasily at times during these past five years when they were reminded of the wrong they had once done Nathan Blaine. Now they were showing a respect to Nathan in death that they could not have brought themselves to express when he was alive.

But that was only a small part of it, the marshal realized. As a matter of cold fact, Nathan had saved the town a great loss in money when he had stopped the robbery.

That was the important thing. Many of these people would have lost their life's savings if the robbery had been carried off. It was a matter of dollars and cents, more than a matter of conscience, that made them look at Nate Blaine in a newer and cleaner light.

And besides, those dark eyes that had blazed in life were now dull in death. They inspired no fear; it wasn't difficult to be charitable to a man when there was no reason to fear him.

Still, Elec was surprised that so many had come to the cemetery that day. Sam Baxter, Bert Surratt, Widow Harper, old Seth Lewellen, all had come to discharge a debt of one sort or another, but they didn't display any sense of loss.

Several cowhands from the big cattle outfits had come out of curiosity, and the new banker and his wife for obvious reasons. Todd Wintworth, now a rising young businessman, seemed uneasy and reluctant as he stood near the edge of the crowd beside his sister.

Amy, Elec noticed, held herself like a proud young queen, ignoring the glances of the curious, her anxious eyes fixed on Jeff Blaine's drawn young face.

"*Dust to dust* . . ." the preacher chanted solemnly, and the marshal shifted his gaze to Wirt and Beulah Sewell, who stood alone on the lower slope, away from the crowd. Wirt looked down at his boots, but Beulah had her small, dull eyes fixed determinedly on the preacher. Elec wondered what thoughts were in her mind.

The marshal finally focused his attention on young Jeff Blaine. There beside the grave, the boy stood rigid and cold. There was the look of brittleness about him, and suppressed violence. His eyes, brilliant and dry, gazed fiercely at some indefinite point in the distance.

Has he learned anything from his pa? Elec wondered. By rights the boy should be in jail right now. Legally, young Blaine was as guilty as Somerson and Fay, and in his tougher days Elec Blasingame would not have argued the fact. But now he had grown soft. An old man stubbornly refusing to face reality.

Tomorrow, he thought bleakly, I'll turn my badge over to Kirk Logan; he's wanted it for a long time. I don't want to be there when young Blaine leaves the track again.

Then a quiet murmur was heard along the slope and Elec realized that the funeral was over. The preacher closed the Bible and walked slowly toward Jeff, but the boy stood like stone, his savage gaze fixed on the distance. The preacher shuffled uncomfortably, started to extend his hand, then changed his mind. At last he murmured something and moved uneasily away.

The crowd milled silently, uncertainly, now that the service was over. A few of them started toward Jeff, but they fell back immediately when they saw the grim cast of his face. They looked at each other uncertainly and finally began drifting away.

Now the congregation began breaking up quickly, as though it had suddenly realized its motive for coming. Cow-hands rounded up their horses. Townspeople brought up buggies and hacks. A grim procession quickly formed and moved hurriedly down the slope toward the town.

Only a few were left now. Even the gravediggers, feeling the strange chill hovering over the hillside, quickly completed their work and went away. Marshal Blasingame held his ground, waiting. Amy Wintworth had not moved, despite her brother's urgent pulling at her arm. And near the bottom of the slope stood Wirt and Beulah Sewell, and Elec could not imagine why those two had stayed.

There they stood, the five of them, and the boy whose face was chiseled in grief. Then, with great effort, Jeff Blaine drew his gaze from the distance and glanced at the marshal. He looked down at the mound of clay, then up at the endless sky.

Jeff looked at the marshal and smiled so slightly that it was hardly discernible. "He said once," Jeff said, "that hate got to be a heavy load, when you couldn't put it down."

Elec thought, So that's what he was thinking. He said, "So you learned something, after all. I didn't think you would."

Elec was the last one to leave, for he had learned some things himself and wanted to think about them carefully. He had believed that man's destiny was a one-way track, immovable as a mountain, unrelenting as steel. He had believed that death was written in the circumstance of birth, and all that happened in between was unimportant, for the end was certain.

Now he wondered, as he watched Amy Wintworth run across the slope, as he saw the look in Jeff Blaine's eyes as he held the girl hard against him. Elec noted Todd Wintworth's helpless anger and was quietly pleased because it was so helpless. And he saw the quick glance exchanged between Beulah Sewell and her husband.

This is the real test, he thought, when Jeff and Amy started down the slope toward them.

It was not an easy thing — that much was clear, even from a distance. But hate got to be a heavy load, when you couldn't put it down. Elec gazed down to where Jeff had paused before his aunt, and the very air seemed to vibrate for a moment. But when the boy made himself speak to Beulah — when he took Wirt's hand, no matter how reluctantly — the marshal knew that Nathan had taught his lesson well.